PLANET OF OUTCASTS

MOON CRUSHER PART 2

SUSAN KITE

This is a work of fiction. Names, characters, places, and incidents are products of the author's imagination or are used fictitiously and are not to be construed as real. Any resemblance to actual events, locations, organizations, or persons, living or dead, is entirely coincidental.

World Castle Publishing, LLC
Pensacola, Florida
Copyright © 2024 Susan Kite
Hardback ISBN: 9798322064978
Paperback ISBN: 9798891261907
eBook ISBN: 9798891261914
First Edition World Castle Publishing, LLC, May 6, 2024
http://www.worldcastlepublishing.com
Licensing Notes
Cover: Cover Designs by Karen
Cover-designs-by-karen.com
Editor: Karen Fuller

I dedicate this book to my Oklahoma critique group, Shelley White, Richard McClellan, Christina Rost, Nelda Holliman-Paden, and Anna Fauntez, all marvelous authors in their own right. They stuck through Moon Crusher 2 and 3. Again; I thank my beloved husband, Dan, for putting up with all this writing over the years.

CHAPTER ONE

Diego studied the input monitors, flashing information faster than he could read it. He was in a surveillance starfighter within the contested system. Resh warlords had built a massive outpost on Luretor Nine, the outermost planet of the Luretor system. Suddenly, an alarm sounded in his ears. Three small Luretor spacecraft converged on Diego's ship. He had stayed too long spying on the Resh outpost. He had also neglected to keep his shields up.

Diego felt the shields distorted the information he was trying to gather, so it was a delicate dance trying to stay hidden and to spy. Diego set the engines to full power. Obviously, it was time to leave.

With a force that shoved him back into the padded seat, the little ship swooped farther out into the depths of space between one system and another. There was nothing to hide behind here, no refuge from the enemy. He would have to stand and fight while he could do some damage. Diego accelerated the starboard engines, pushing him back again while spinning his ship behind the enemy fighters.

He realized his ship could take out two of the enemy, but which two? And what in the world was he going to do about the third fighter? He glanced at his monitor, trying to do the instant calculations to decide. A chirp in his headset told him his time was up. With a touch on the handset, he fired two laser blasts.

Diego didn't wait to see if he was successful or not. He shoved the controls forward to avoid enemy fire. His brain told him he was traveling straight down, but he had been told there was no 'up or down' in space. Too bad, his brain responded — it was down.

Diego rolled his ship as he checked the monitor. One of his enemies was gone, destroyed by his weaponry. With a dissatisfied growl, Diego studied the monitor while keeping his hand on the weapon controls. There! He fired. Another ship disappeared in a quick flash. Now for the last one. He banked left, keeping watch on the other Resh ship. It wasn't on the monitor! Where was it, he wondered, ordering the computer to find it.

A flash and a violent shuddering told him the enemy had scored on him.

He sighed as the controls became dark and the outside lights brightened. Diego Perez, squire to Commander Ziron, a high-ranking officer in the Seressin Empire, wondered how in the world he had defeated three Resh star cruisers in an actual battle almost six months ago. He concluded as he had before, that he had a great deal of help and a lot of luck.

With another sigh, he slid out of his seat in the simulator to face the flight leader, Commander Weelix, a very formidable wolf-like Breanth. "Give me your assessment of this exercise, Quirlis Diego."

"I was defeated, Rejas," Diego said bluntly.

"Can you assess what defeated you?" growled Weelix. His numerous sharp teeth in an elongated snout made him look fierce, but his golden eyes studied Diego with no hostility.

Diego thought. There were ten students in the class, and none said anything while Diego considered. This was very unlike his first class after his selection as Commander Ziron's squire. "I didn't use my shielding devices correctly, which allowed the enemy to detect me and keep me from bringing back my information."

"Do you think you got more information by waiting overly

long—and with your shields down?" Weelix asked.

"Yes, Rejas."

"Did that information do the Seressin Empire any good?"

Diego sighed again. "No, Rejas Weelix. I couldn't get back with the information."

"Couldn't the information have been sent in a message burst?" Rreengrol, Diego's close friend, asked, his green eyes round in their concern.

Diego gave himself a mental slap. "Knowing I was in a dangerous situation, I should have sent back the critical information."

Weelix nodded. "However, the good news is that you did better with your piloting skills. Are the systems becoming a little easier to use, Quirlis?"

Diego realized that the computers and other electronic systems were getting easier to figure out. "Yes, sir!"

"That is what we look for with the simulation. Improvement. Rishtez, you are next," Weelix said to a young Seressin squire.

Several more squires went through the simulator exercises before Weelix dismissed the class.

"You are getting better, Diego Treshtura-lun," Rreengrol said, slapping his friend on the back, using his newly acquired warrior name—Moon Crusher.

Rreengrol was a Grrlock, a creature with a light pelt of fur, a tail, and very cat-like features. He had been one of the very few squires in the early days who had been his friend. Rreengrol had been patient with him, and he was the one who had given Marix Ziron the idea for the new name.

Diego let his mind wander back to that time.

***

"How does it feel to be a sub-commander, Quirlis Diego?" Commander Ziron boomed after the ceremony where Diego had been promoted. A heavy reptilian hand slapped him on the back, and Diego almost fell forward.

"Not to mention a Moon Crusher, Marix," Rreengrol added, standing just in front of his commander, Hreeshan, the highest ranking Grrlock in the Seressin Empire. They also promoted Rreengrol to the position of sub-commander.

Diego started. The Seressin word Rreengrol used was Treshtura-lun. It was somewhat like the Spanish equivalent trituradora de luna.

"Treshtura-lun," Ziron said thoughtfully. "That is a good Seressin warrior's name. That will have to be placed on the rolls."

And it was.

***

Several more sessions in the flight simulator had Diego thinking he might just be mastering the art of piloting the one and two seat starfighters. Of course, with another crew member, one could split the duties, thus making it easier. Diego's favorite partner was Rreengrol, although any of the other squires in this class were good partners.

Still, sometimes Diego wished he had his favorite gelding and was riding over the hills and valleys of his homeland. He had checked in the library for any worlds that had creatures resembling horses and hills, like his father's land. There was plenty of the latter, but those devilish-looking creatures he had fought on Koress were the closest animals to horses he had found. Diego quit looking.

Recently, Commander Ziron had selected another squire, a young Breanth named Wengr, from Commander Weelix's den. Diego had relinquished his mealtime duties after the marix had picked the Breanth. Diego swore Ziron seemed determined for him to pilot a starship before he was sixteen. At least that was Diego's consensus after a lengthy day where he had attended a full day of classes and then stood a watch on the bridge, not only observing the various duty stations but taking a turn at each one.

That night, when he returned to his cabin, Diego gazed into the narrow mirror in his tiny bathroom. He saw dark brown eyes staring back at him, eyes different from almost any other creature on the ship. His brown hair was cut short. While he normally liked to wear it longer, long hair was too difficult to keep out of his face during training. Diego noticed that his skin was lighter than when the Seressin had captured him. You got little sunlight on a spaceship, and it had been almost a half-year cycle since he had been on Koress. His nose was narrow, again something totally different from the other species on board the *Star Devourer*. He had no fangs, no hard skin, fur, or scales, and no real claws. What in the world did Commander Ziron see in him when he and his sub-commanders landed on his planet?

With a sigh, Diego turned away. A ferocious yawn told him he was too tired to shower. Another yawn sent him to collapse onto his narrow bed. He was asleep almost immediately.

CHAPTER TWO

A sickly colored, roiling fog curled around his boots. Diego gazed upward and saw the same oppressive yellow brown in the sky as he had seen on Koress. The clouds were black, but not with rain. Several creatures strode up, stopping two horse-lengths in front of him. They were thin and tall, with stick-like limbs. The limbs and body were jointed in strange ways, almost like praying mantises from Earth. Koressian diplomats. Diego remembered some of those on Koress when Commander Ziron and others were trying to negotiate with the Koressian leaders. It was when those same leaders were also negotiating with the toad-like Resh, enemy to the Seressin.

They chittered in their clacking language, waving their stick-like hands in the air.

Diego was wearing his martial arts workout uniform without a translator or weapons. "I can't understand you."

The Koressians paused, and one made a motion at the narrow part of its body that served as a waist. "Can you understand us now?"

"Yes." Diego looked around quickly to find Marix Ziron. There seemed to be no one else nearby. He heard no calls for help or greeting.

"Do not look for your companions to help you. It is you we want."

Diego realized asking why was foolish. He knew why, so he said nothing.

"You and your commander have ruined our world."

Diego shook his head. "You did that. By choosing to betray

us...." *The Koressians disappeared. Not even the fog swirled. A banging he thought he'd never hear again filled the air. In the distance, Diego saw the Koressian desert warriors on their fearsome horse-like beasts. He counted six of them, and they were all beating their gunstocks on a metal plate on their saddles. Then, the creatures shot forward like bullets from percussion pistols. The beasts screamed, their long, sharp teeth bared.*

Diego looked around for anything to use against these fighters, knowing that it was useless. How did I get here? And why? *He saw a large club and snatched it up. It was scant defense against such fearsome fighters, but better than nothing.*

Still, he ducked beneath the spear of the first, grabbed the outstretched arm, and jerked the warrior from his saddle. That surprised him, but then two of the warriors fired their weapons at him and missed. That surprised him even more.

The warrior on the ground leaped for him, but Diego was ready, knocking him away with the club. Then, the riderless beast came at him. It didn't slow down, attempting to trample him with its hooves, so Diego crouched, ready to spring. His timing was perfect as he sprang into the saddle. The beast reared, but Diego clamped his legs tight against the saddle, gathering the metal-link reins in one hand and jerking out a scimitar-like sword from a scabbard built into the saddle.

Two of the warriors came for him, aiming their weapons. Leaning low against the beast's neck, Diego kicked it into a gallop. Apparently, that wasn't how these riders guided their mounts. The creature screamed and reached around to bite him. Diego used his fist on its rough-skinned snout, wincing at the pain from his bloody knuckles.

That seemed to be the right move, as the 'horse' took off in the direction he wanted it to go. The wind whistled past his ears and made his eyes water. Diego felt strangely exhilarated despite the differences between this animal and the horses he had grown up around all his life. "¡Arre!" he shouted. "¡Arre!" Diego was astonished when the creature ran even faster.

Then he looked ahead and saw a line of machines, as well as more creatures. The warriors on their backs banged their weapons. The machines made high-pitched whining noises. Searing light flashed and….

Diego jerked out of bed, his covers wrapped around his body, sweat dripping down the side of his face. The lights came partially on, telling him it was still the middle of the sleep period. Nothing else was in his room. Diego pulled the blanket off and glanced down. He was still in his uniform.

With a sigh, Diego pulled off the sweat-soaked coverall and took a quick shower. Then he pulled on his pajamas and sat on his bed. Putting in the earplugs, Diego lay down and listened to the gentle flow of the computer teacher, Anaar's voice, teaching him more words in the Seressin language. Somehow, this form of teaching also provided him with the symbols for the words as well. However, it worked, Diego was glad. It was a lot easier than trying to memorize everything the way he had learned Latin in Father Antonio's class. He fell asleep hearing Anaar's voice teaching.

***

Commander Ziron stood away from the chart he and Diego had been studying. The Seressin exhaled heavily, then bent close to Diego and bared his razor-sharp teeth. The reptilian ship commander's blue cheek patches shone brightly, whether with anger or disgust, Diego couldn't discern. He knew Marix Ziron was not happy. He was having trouble remembering the various names and places on the chart. The Seressin's thick tail lashed from side to side. "Who would have thought you conceived and led an attack on the enemy only a scant hundred cycles ago? Not just once, but three times!" Ziron growled. "Perhaps we were both dreaming!"

"Marix, I…I didn't sleep well last night. I kept seeing things from the past. What could have been when I saw you and the others dying. I don't know why because we changed that outcome." Diego sucked in a deep breath. "I know I should never apologize, but despite your victory, I keep wondering when the Resh are coming again. And I wonder if I might yet fail you." Diego bowed his head. He would never have admitted such a thing when Ziron had first chosen him to be the commander's squire. However, having saved the commander's life, as well as several other high-ranking Seressin commanders, Ziron had been more considerate of his squire's well-being the past month-cycles.

"You dreamed of the Resh?"

"Not last night, but I have recently."

"I will check with the spies and with Seressin intelligence. Right now, that is the best we can do, but let me know if you have more of these dreams."

"Yes, Commander."

"You are a sub-commander, even as you are still my senior squire. It is good you continue to serve as my squire. You are not quite ready for a command. You still have much to learn." Ziron drew back and thought, his eyes looking toward the ceiling. "I do not say that against your abilities. Your people seem complicated, and you learn differently. I feel you will be great someday. Still, I have never heard of this kind of thing you are describing. Perhaps it is something that afflicts mammalians. Your dreams saved our lives before, but too much interrupted sleep is also dangerous. Do you think they will go away?"

"I don't know, Marix. I only want to serve you, and I dislike feeling this way."

Ziron scratched under his chin with a clawed index finger.

When Diego first entered Ziron's service, such consideration was unthinkable among any Seressin, much less the Lord Commander of a Seressin starship. The boy felt hesitant to admit even this much.

"Diego, put away the charts. Then go find Commander Hreeshan and send him to me. Spend some time with the other squires. It is almost free time."

"Yes, Marix." With a sigh, he rolled up the charts, which contained statistics of several Seressin allies and enemies, then put them in a special cabinet inset in Ziron's cabin wall. By calling his second in command, Ziron was contemplating replacing him. "I continue to serve you, Lord Ziron, in whatever capacity," Diego intoned with a bow before heading for the door of the commander's exercise room.

As though reading his mind, Ziron barked, "By the comet, I am not replacing you, nor do I plan on having you for dinner, Quirlis. You are too valuable. I want you able to serve as you did those hundred cycles ago!"

"Yes, Marix." Diego sighed again as he slid out the door.

It didn't take him long to find Hreeshan. He was drilling new squires in the martial arts room.

"Here." The Grrlock commander shoved a very plain but heavy sword toward the young man. Hreeshan was cat-like with pointed ears high on his head, whiskers which flicked in curiosity, a soft layer of short fur, and a tail held straight behind him. "You are capable. Show these new squires the Krillian defensive moves," Hreeshan ordered. "And then dismiss them."

"Yes, Rejas."

Hreeshan swept out of the room, and Diego turned to see ten pairs of eyes on him. There were a few Seressin youths, one Grrlock, a Breanth, even a few Turengen, as well as two beings unknown to him. Diego exchanged the heavier sword for a lighter one. Despite his fatigue, he showed the moves specified by Hreeshan. After a few moments, he asked, "Would anyone like to try these moves against me?"

"Me!" one of the Turengen called out. She jumped forward with her sword thrust out. Diego parried it away from his lower legs. Turengen, who resembled overgrown otters, stood thigh high.

"Very well," he said. Diego knew how fierce these

little creatures were, but he still felt the short being was at a disadvantage. He needn't have. The creature's speed made up for her stature, and Diego found himself practicing the defensive moves more than he had expected. The Turengen darted in and out, making the defensive moves into offensive moves. Diego even felt the prick of the end of the blade on his ankle as the little being wove between his legs and behind him. With great effort, Diego finally knocked the blade from the Turengen's paw.

"What is your name?" Diego asked when he finally had breath. "That was a very good adaptation of the moves, by the way."

"Fress, Commander Diego. Younger sister to Groosh. Groosh was a warrior. I will also be a warrior."

Diego couldn't help it, even in his fatigue, he smiled. "I suspect you will, Fress. Groosh was a very brave warrior." Before he dismissed them, Diego asked the other new squires for their names. All cleaned and stored their weapons and then filed out of the training room. The Turengen stayed behind, their bright eyes gazing into his face. Knowing their ability to read minds, he didn't doubt they were concerned about his tiredness.

"Commander..." Grash began.

"I am still a squire," Diego corrected him, uncomfortable with being called commander.

"You are commander," Pesh, another female, corrected him. "You were promoted. Twice."

Diego sighed.

"Our grandsires might be able to help you with bad memories, with your nightmares, Commander," Merff, a male, announced.

Diego expected several Turengen comments, but that wasn't one of them. "What?"

"Yes, sir. Our grandsires learned from their grandsires. The grandsires helped some other captured beings," Merff added.

Maybe that was another reason Diego had liked the otter

people. "How do they do it?"

"Not sure," Fress said, "But we can ask during free time."

Diego hesitated. He felt he should be stronger than this. That he should take care of his own problems, but if he was a danger to his marix… "I don't know."

The Turengen gazed at him, and then they all pattered out as Rreengrol entered the training room. "I was wondering where you were. Let's get something to eat. It's mid-meal."

Diego was ready to skip the meal and go to his room to get a nap, but his stomach overruled him. It growled loudly.

Rreengrol scratched behind an ear, trying to hide a grin. "Let's go eat. Then you can nap."

"You a mind reader like the Turengen?"

"No, you just have the look of someone who has missed a few hours of sleep."

"A few."

"Care to tell me about it?"

Diego appreciated the concern, but it began grating on his nerves. Even Lord Ziron had been kind. Seressins were not normally kind. They were tough and admired toughness. "No," he growled. "Not now."

Rreengrol shrugged. "The commanders have noticed."

"I know!" Diego said in a voice louder than he wanted. Several other squires gazed at him before continuing down the corridor. "Sorry, Rreengrol. I already said something to Lord Ziron, and he has undoubtedly spoken to Commander Hreeshan about it."

"What did Marix Ziron say, if I may ask?"

"He seemed concerned, but I don't think Seressins have this kind of problem. They don't seem to be bothered by nightmares that make them wonder if what they are doing is right."

Rreengrol shook his head. "I think Lord Ziron thinks of you as a soft-skinned son."

Diego stopped and gaped at him. He had several ideas

about his changed status with Ziron, but a son? He couldn't think of one thing to say, so he continued down the corridor.

They entered the serving area, where a dozen others ate. "We can talk later," Diego muttered.

"All right."

The food here was even better than he had enjoyed when he was first selected by the ship's commander. Still, despite his growling stomach, he chose little. Diego picked an empty table, and Rreengrol joined him after filling up his tray.

"You need a vacation," Rreengrol said before he started on his mid-meal.

"What?"

"You need to get off the ship. Take leave. Get some fresh air. Have fun. We're squires, fledging sub-commanders, not machines."

"Leave? Sounds nice, but where and how?"

Rreengrol shrugged and took a bite of his meat patty. "How about coming home with me on my next leave?"

"Seriously? When is that?"

"I have requested next Moon-day."

"What's Moon-day?"

"It's a mid-summer holiday when the moon is in an extra-long dark phase. There are lots of fun things to do. At the very least, you'll be able to relax. We have some of the best mountain exploration areas in the galaxy where we can camp, explore, fish, even hunt. Commander Hreeshan is taking leave then, too. He has been away from his life-mate too long. I'm going on the same shuttle he is."

"How do I go about getting this leave?"

"Get on a computer and fill out the form. I can help you."

"I don't know if Marix Ziron will let me."

"Never know until you ask," Rreengrol said, shoving another bite of meat into his mouth. "Now eat. That meager little cub portion is probably cold by now."

Diego smiled and took a bite. Rreengrol was right. It was cold.

CHAPTER THREE

Buzzing woke Diego from a deep sleep. It was like an angry hornet creeping up his chest. In his half-sleep, the young man tried to brush it away. His hand grasped a small pin attached magnetically to his sleeping attire. It occurred to him what he was hearing. It was a summons from Marix Ziron.

Jumping out of bed, Diego threw on his ship's uniform, practically leaped into his boots, and placed the communicator on the outside of his tunic. "I am almost there, Marix." He glanced at his clock, which showed it was almost first-meal. He couldn't believe he had slept so late.

The tiny cabins suited the most junior of the junior officers. There was a narrow bed that folded to become a chair for the tiny desk across from it. The room was incredibly minuscule. Still, it was a place to sleep, and last night, he had fallen asleep quickly and slept soundly, untroubled by dreams.

A final buzz told the squire Ziron had heard him. It didn't tell him if the Seressin was angry or not. Diego sealed the edges of the uniform fastenings as he dashed toward the marix's quarters. This time, he was well versed with the route. He also didn't have to worry about waking a roommate. A sub-commander, even one of the lowest rank and job description, had his own cabin.

His hand brushed the identity plate next to the commander's door. It slid open immediately. Ziron sat at his desk. There was no sign of the junior squire.

"A half-minute later than last time," Ziron barked. He leaned over the desk where Diego had come to attention. "At least you look more rested than you did yesterday afternoon."

"Yes, Marix."

"No dreams?"

"No, sir. Maybe they will stop now."

"Perhaps, perhaps not. Remember, advise me of any dreams that seem important to you. The one on Koress saved the empire."

"Yes, sir."

"You have been on my ship for almost a Seressin year, half of that time under my direct command. Considering your background, you have done extremely well." His sharp teeth gleamed as he smiled.

Diego blushed and ducked his head briefly before returning his gaze to his commander's penetrating orange-red eyes. "Thank you, Marix. My only ambition is...."

Ziron waved his taloned hand. "To serve me. I know. Few of my own kind can be counted so loyal." He straightened up and drew in a deep breath. "I would like you to accompany Commander Hreeshan to his Grrlock home world during his leave. My understanding is that he is also taking his squire with him. You may take one of the younger squires with you."

Diego's jaw dropped. "Marix?"

"Don't make me repeat myself, or I may change my mind!"

"Yes, Marix! Thank you!"

"You will come back rested and fit because by then, I might be ready to decapitate my junior squire. Besides, in thirty cycles, we will head out on an important assignment."

"Yes, sir!" He continued to stand as straight as a pike.

Ziron huffed. "You are dismissed. Commander Hreeshan and his squire will leave at last meal today, so you have little time. Make sure you let Commander Lurin know which squire you have selected."

"Thank you, Marix!" Diego walked from the commander's cabin with as much decorum as possible, but as soon as he was in the corridor, he sprinted to his room. Three weeks to relax and see a planet where the people were friendly. No fighting, no training, no stress, no classes.

Rreengrol stood in front of his cabin door, a big grin on his face. "You want some help packing?"

"Packing what? I have nothing except my uniforms and workout outfits." Diego swallowed. He couldn't wear a uniform on leave.

"I thought as much. What have you been doing with your stipends?"

"Stipends?"

Rreengrol sighed, but Diego could detect a bit of a purr deep in his throat. "My friend, once you were no longer a slave, you were on the payroll as part of the crew."

"You mean I have been paid for the past half year?"

"You should have been. We can check on the computer for that, too."

"Lord Ziron said something about taking a squire to help me on my leave."

Rreengrol shrugged. "Even a sub-commander must keep up pretenses. Someone to help you with, uh, personal items, I suppose."

"You mean like a slave to help me with clothes and the like?"

"Well, in the old days, you'd have had a slave to help you, but there's been a little progress lately." Rreengrol chuckled. "Well, who do you want to share this adventure with?"

Diego opened his cabin door and motioned Rreengrol to enter. "Have a seat wherever you can find one."

He sat down on the end of the bunk and drew up his legs. "Who are you picking?"

Diego sat in the remaining space. "I'd like to take Bress,

but last I heard, he was thoroughly enjoying training young covert warriors. Still, I want to take a Turengen."

"How about one of the new squires?"

"All right, I'll take Fress. She is unafraid but is also smart."

"You'll need to let her know soon so she can prepare."

"And tell Commander Lurin, too."

"Let's send a message to Fress, then go eat. You can tell Lurin after the meal. We'll also get you something other than a uniform from the ship's stores."

***

After first-meal, Diego barely had a chance to summon Fress before Rreengrol dragged him off to a clothing distribution room. This one was bigger than the one Phris, his first mentor, had taken him to after his capture, and the creature behind the counter was friendlier, even though it was stranger.

Arms reached up from the top of its head or body. Eyes blinked at him from the middle of its torso. The bright green skin warred with the orange and pink patches of fur down its sides. A box hung just above its eyes. A soft voice came from the box. "What is it you need, young Commander?"

Diego looked around, then realized the alien was speaking to him. It was still hard to realize that he was a sub-commander. He glanced at Rreengrol.

"You do not have a pelt, and the nights are cold, so you will need a mountain jacket of the third degree, hiking boots, mitts. You will also need several pairs of leisure outfits." Rreengrol ticked off each item on his fingers.

"What?" Diego choked. "But...."

Rreengrol shook his head and sighed. "Kor-lung, can you check on the status of our friend's budget?"

"Yes," the box said. Kor-lung's arms reached in front of him and tapped on what Diego assumed was a computer. There was a pause and more tapping. Another pause, and then, "There is more than enough to outfit Sub-Commander Diego Perez for a furlough on Grrlock." Seeing Diego's shocked look, he added. "And plenty left over for more excursions."

"But how? All those kinds of things would take many seamstresses on my world and much time."

"Diego, my friend," Rreengrol purred. "You first received a bonus for the defeat of the Resh and the Koressians. Then you got bounties for the destruction of several Resh ships, plus a sub-commander's salary. You, my friend, are a very well-to-do Seressin citizen. I heard a High Commander added to the bonuses, too. So quit your stuttering, and let's get you outfitted." Rreengrol gazed at Kor-lung and added, "Do you have similar supplies for a Turengen female?"

"Of course. Turengen do not need as many layers. They have a pelt like you. And are smaller. By the way, young Turengen or old one?"

"Young," Diego answered. That was the only thing he was sure of right now.

Kor-lung oozed through a door behind him. Diego didn't see legs. They waited. While they stood waiting, the door to the supply room slid open, and Fress pattered in.

"Thank you, Commander. You are most kind to consider me as a helper on the planet of Sub-Commander Rreengrol. I will be loyal, helpful, and brave."

Rreengrol gave a throaty chuckle. "We are both still squires. It would not be fitting to call us commanders around those of higher rank."

"Perhaps not, but you were given that rank," she reminded them.

"Yes, but we're too young to use them properly," Diego said, wishing she'd drop the subject.

She did but gazed at him, her eyes sad. Diego realized he had invited someone who could pick up his feelings, and he blushed.

"Will do my best not to intrude."

"You'll be fine," Diego reassured her. "And you're coming to have fun, too."

"See what you think of these, Sub-Commander Diego Perez," Kor-lung wheezed. There was a pile of clothes and supplies on the counter.

Rreengrol picked up part of the pile. "Let me help you take these to a private room while Fress waits for her things."

Diego grabbed the rest, wondering how in the world Kor-lung managed all of this by himself.

Rreengrol pulled out a one-piece outfit that looked similar to a uniform in design but without the rank or work designation. "You shouldn't have to try this on; just see if you like it. I guarantee it will fit."

Diego was still trying to get used to his newfound wealth. "I like it. It's not as gaudy as a uniform and looks very comfortable."

"How about this one?" Rreengrol held up another one. He continued until they went through six different outfits.

Then he handed Diego the jacket. He tried it on and felt almost like he was wrapped in a quilt, except not as restrictive.

By the time they had looked at, tried on, and examined everything Kor-lung brought out, Fress had finished. She had all her things in a container on wheels that followed her around like a puppy.

A similar but larger container sat in front of the counter. "Do I put all of my new clothes in it?" Diego asked.

Rreengrol nodded. Soon, the three were heading out of the supply room. "I'll take your belongings to my cabin. You need to let Commander Lurin know about Fress's leave."

Diego nodded.

"Take mine, too?" Fress asked.

Rreengrol nodded. "Yes, I can." He clapped his hands and turned away. The wheeled cases followed him like miniature carriages without horses.

CHAPTER FOUR

Commander Lurin's quarters were no longer below decks, but he roomed away from most of the senior commanders and their squires. When Diego and Fress had gone down two elevators and many corridors, he pressed his hand against the raised plate that identified visitors to an individual's cabin. Like most things on the huge starship, he didn't understand how it worked, only that it did.

The door slid open, and Diego and Fress entered.

Lurin stood over a large and extremely cluttered table. Printed charts lay in one corner, loose machine parts holding down the edges. Some kind of contraption stood in the middle, metal parts and wires jutting out in a variety of directions. A small wheel spun slowly on one side of the apparatus.

"Unless you can suggest something to make this piece of junk work, state your purpose for being here and then leave!" Lurin snapped.

Diego wasn't sure if Lurin was angry at them or the machine or just being his usual grumpy self. Fress nudged him on the leg. "Uh, Rejas. I have leave on Grrlock, and Marix Ziron told me to pick a junior squire to accompany me."

Lurin banged a piece of metal on the table and turned to gaze at him. "So?"

"The Commander said to tell you when I made my choice, Rejas."

"And you decided to take a Turengen, probably one of my most valuable students."

"Uh, yes, sir. But if…"

"By the comet, you deserve a bit of time away from all this. I assume you decided on this young fur-ball." He pointed to Fress.

"Yes, Commander."

Fress climbed up on the table, found a part, and handed it to Lurin. "Put it there, Rejas. Will work better." She pointed at the spinning wheel side of the contraption.

Lurin stared at her in surprise. "Yes, that is logical. Not sure why you Turengen weren't tapped as mechanical squires and technical trainees long ago." He turned to Diego. "Make sure you bring Squire Fress back in one piece."

"Yes, Rejas. I promise."

"You and Hreeshan's squire make sure you also make it back."

"Oh, we will, Rejas."

Lurin had already turned back to his work. Fress hopped down off the table, and she and Diego left. They headed to Rreengrol's cabin, but an old Turengen stood in the middle of the corridor in front of the elevator. At least Diego assumed she was older. White streaks mingled with the dark brown of her pelt.

"You come with me," she said, pointing to Diego.

He gazed at Fress. She shrugged. "I said I would talk to the grands."

"I have to meet my friend. There isn't much time," Diego protested.

"Your friend will not leave you," she said, beckoning for him to follow her. She chittered to Fress, who scampered into the elevator.

Diego had no choice but to follow. She led him through several corridors, down an elevator, and several more corridors. The old Turengen reached a door, slid her hand over a low ident plate. The door slid open, and a cacophony of loud chittering, some screeching, and the clattering of many toenails greeted him as he ducked his head to enter the room.

"Kids are restless," the grandmother Turengen said, beckoning Diego to follow her.

Several of the younger otter people stopped and stared at him, then most resumed whatever they were doing, which appeared to be chaos.

"In here, Commander."

"I'm a squire, Grandmother."

"And I am called Cril Merme."

She was the first Turengen he had met who had more than a one-syllable name. Perhaps only the old ones received longer names, he thought. She held back a roughly woven cloth covering the entrance to an alcove about the size of his cabin.

"Sit, sit."

He sat. The sooner he cooperated, the sooner he could get out of here and back to Rreengrol's cabin.

"Your thoughts are those of someone who has seen more than good for a person your age."

"If you count my capture, I guess so."

She nodded. "That is so." Cril Merme sat back and hummed with her eyes closed. Diego waited, growing impatient. Then, just as he was ready to interrupt her meditation, he relaxed. It was like he was beside a flowing river among lush hills. Birds trilled, and insects rustled. Otters, real otters, not Turengen, zipped under the water, occasionally leaping above the surface and then splashing back under. There was a chirp in his ear, and he realized his eyes had been closed. Diego opened them. He felt very relaxed and wondered if he had dozed off.

"No. Did not sleep. Just found something peaceful in your mind. Remember that place. Use it when you are anxious. Use it before going to sleep at night."

"That's it?" In a way, Diego was a little disappointed. He

expected medicine or…or something.

"You use something pleasant until the unpleasant becomes memories of when you were brave, sure, and confident in yourself and others."

"And I do it before I go to sleep?"

"Yes, then dreams will be better."

"What if I have a foretelling dream?"

She stared into his eyes. "You will tell the difference."

"Thank you."

"You go now before Grrlock sub-commander comes for you."

"Oh, sure. Uh, Cril Merme, could one of the young ones guide me to the upper levels? I think I might have gotten turned around coming down here."

She chittered happily. "Of course." Before the words had left her mouth, a small Turengen with a light-colored pelt popped into the old Turengen's room. "Be safe. Come back with my great-niece."

"Yes, señora."

With the help of the small otter person, Diego was soon at Rreengrol's cabin.

"About time you showed up. We only have a little time before we report to the transport."

Fress and the luggage were nowhere to be seen. "Where are—"

"I sent the luggage ahead."

"What?" Diego wasn't sure he liked the idea of someone else dealing with his stuff.

"What we forget, we can grab on Grrlock. Let's go. I'd rather be early than have Hreeshan wondering what kept us," Rreengrol said with a hint of a toothy smile.

Diego felt excitement building. He grinned back. "Let's go, then."

Soon they were in a large shuttle bay where several

spacecraft waited. In front of the largest one stood Hreeshan, talking with a Seressin pilot. Diego recognized Prengi, the Seressin who had piloted during the battle of Koress, standing next to an older Seressin.

"Surprises keep falling out of trees," Rreengrol murmured. He waited until Hreeshan nodded to them and then turned to the younger Seressin. "Are you piloting us?"

Prengi shook his head, giving them a broad smile, a greeting that would scare a timid creature half to death. Seressin's teeth were sharp and numerous. "No, I am the second pilot. I wanted to see your world and was offered a few days' furlough. Plus, this gives me the experience of helping pilot a long-range transport."

"Great!" Diego replied. "Not that you need any more experience as an apprentice pilot."

"Thanks. Why don't you two get on board? Diego, your squire is already settled."

Rreengrol sat to the left of Hreeshan, and Diego was on Rreengrol's left. Fress scrunched down in the aisle seat next to Diego. Small monitors on the back of the seats in front of them showed the shuttle bay. Buttons on his armrest changed the view on the screen so Diego could see outside, much like the High Commander's shuttle had shown him views all around the ship, near and far. Diego kept twisting the button to see what was available.

One channel told him about Grrlock, and Diego watched this one for a while, seeing what landforms the planet had. There were several mountain ranges, two oceans, and a few smaller seas. Some mountains were so tall, they were wreathed in clouds, and the tallest one carpeted in snow. The lakes were a blue-violet color, with ice ringing their shores.

"We're going to that one," Rreengrol pointed to one of them.

"Looks cold," Diego replied.

"We came prepared."

Diego nodded and continued gazing at the monitor as it changed to another part of the planet. This time, he was looking at beaches with dark blue sands. The waves lapping the beach were light blue, topped with golden foam. "Wow!" he breathed.

"We'll visit there first if you'd like."

"Yes, if it's not too much trouble."

"I have an uncle who lives near the western ocean."

"By the way, I'm curious about something."

"What?" Rreengrol asked, leaning back into his cushioned chair.

"Why was I required to bring a squire, and you weren't?"

Rreengrol gave a mock sigh. "I don't know why I like you so much. I must explain so many obvious things."

Diego bristled. "Wait a minute!"

Rreengrol laughed. "I am only kidding, but it is obvious."

Knowing how his Grrlock friend liked to tease, Diego waited.

"Three reasons. One—you are Commander Ziron's senior squire, and he likes you. Two, as I said before, he **really** respects you and wanted someone else to look out for you."

"What?" Diego knew the commander had been more solicitous since the battle and knew the Seressin leader was grateful for saving him and the high commanders, but Diego had considered it his duty. He had not expected a promotion out of it, not that he wasn't grateful, especially when that included being given his freedom. To him, that meant more than any of the promotions or the monetary rewards.

"He's always liked you for some strange reason," Rreengrol added with a laugh.

Diego punched him on the shoulder.

"Oh, and the third reason is that I will have my younger sister along. She has applied to become a squire and is hoping to hear about it by the time our leave is over."

Diego continued to watch the tutorial. He wasn't sure about having more and more people on their leave, but he had never been in this situation, so he would not make any judgments right now.

CHAPTER FIVE

The trip took slightly over six hours. The *Star Devourer* had been outside the orbit of the fifth world, so it was an in-system flight. Diego napped, falling asleep during another tutorial about Rreengrol's home. He remembered a brief dream where a Koressian appeared but disappeared as soon as he pulled out a dream sword. Diego assumed that was also the doing of Cril Merme. There was a snack and a drink, both from Grrlock. The snack was all right, but the drink, which reminded him of fermented milk, he set aside.

"Don't want your prensor?" Rreengrol asked in his own language.

He and Rreengrol had practiced the Grrlock language ever since the Battle of Koress, and recently, the Grrlock declared him fluent. Diego shook his head. Rreengrol finished his own drink and had a white mustache under his nose.

"You can have mine." His friend didn't hesitate; he took the proffered drink.

"Is the trip much farther?" Fress asked in a combination of Seressin and Grrlock. Bress had said the Turengen were quick learners.

"No," Hreeshan said. "In fact, Squire, if you turn on your monitor, you can watch the approach."

Fress gazed at the monitor with rapt attention. Diego watched with her. After the battle against the Koressians, being a passenger on a transport was boring. Still, it was a pleasant change.

The cushioning in the seats thickened as they approached the planet. Prengi and his senior pilot made a smooth landing, with only a little buffeting as they entered the atmosphere. The restraints fell away when the engines powered down. Diego stood up, feeling something different.

"Gravity's lighter on my planet," Rreengrol explained. "The Seressin ships have a slightly higher artificial gravity to more closely match what they're used to."

Diego had studied the science of mass, gravity, and physics with Anaar, so he was familiar with what Rreengrol was saying. "That ought to make hiking on your world a little easier."

"With our mountains, that is a scant help."

"I will have to admit I was more used to riding a horse across the grassy hills than hiking up mountain paths. I hope I don't spoil your vacation."

"Don't worry about it. I have been away for a long time, so I'm out of practice."

Diego just smiled. As they exited the transport, they saw their belongings being loaded onto a transport that looked much like a wagon. Diego gazed up and saw pink, puffy clouds rolling across an azure sky. A yellow-orange sun appearing a little bigger than the sun on his birth planet was sitting a handsbreadth above the far horizon. A noise brought his attention back to the ground. Another vehicle pulled behind their luggage transport with a Grrlock beckoning to them. The squires followed Hreeshan. The inside of the vehicle was much more comfortable than Diego thought possible, not a thing like the carriages in his father's stable.

The group rode to a building, appearing to be a gathering place for those coming from space or other parts of Grrlock. A loud yowl caused Rreengrol to jerk around; then he rushed toward an older and larger Grrlock. They cuffed each other on the shoulders, and then what Diego assumed was a female gathered his friend into her arms and rubbed against both cheeks. Diego also assumed these two were Rreengrol's mother and father, but then Rreengrol had alluded to his mother being dead. Perhaps he had misinterpreted what his friend had said before.

"You two will be in good hands," Hreeshan said. "My mate comes…." He broke off to give his attention to a light furred Grrlock. Soon, they were also in each other's arms.

Diego stood next to Fress, wondering what to do next. Finally, Rreengrol beckoned him and Fress over to the family.

"This is my father, Shenell, and my second mother, Lershan," Rreengrol said. He introduced his shipmates and added, "Diego saved mine and Commander Hreeshan's life on Koress. Fress's relatives were part of the assault group as well. Her brother died in that battle."

Lershan grabbed Diego and wrapped her arms around him, doing the same cheek rub on him as she had done to Rreengrol. "You will always be welcome in our denning. Rreengrol told me of the terrible battle."

Diego didn't squirm away, even though he wanted to.

When she let him go, Lershan snatched up Fress and did the same to her. The Turengen squeaked her surprise but didn't pull away either.

"Let us go. There is much to talk about," Shenell said, motioning to the long whiskered Grrlock, who was watching their luggage.

"Where is Rrishan?" Rreengrol asked.

"She is home with Shegrol," Lershan replied.

Rreengrol turned to his two companions. "My younger sister and brother. Rrishan is only a year younger than me and dreams of being a squire, too. Until recently, girls weren't allowed."

"What changed that?"

"That last battle. You know some fighters were female.

Rrishan is going to love Fress."

Fress preened and then said, "Will be glad to meet your sister."

Diego just smiled as they all slid into a large passenger vehicle. He and the other two squires shared a seat. The service Grrlock finished putting all their belongings into the back of the vehicle and pushed a button that caused a covering to close. Shenell stabbed a button, and a switch, and the vehicle growled to a start. It slid into a line of similar transports and then into a wide roadway, with vehicles whizzing in both directions.

After close to a year on Commander Ziron's ship, this kind of openness was a little disconcerting. Then Diego remembered why he was here and relaxed. Everything felt right.

CHAPTER SIX

Diego watched the countryside slide by at a speed that would have boggled his mind a scant year before. They left the spaceport, and the further they traveled, the more the traffic thinned. Fields stretched out from both sides of the road. To the west, Diego saw animals grazing in a field. Long-necked, long-legged quadrupeds feasted on the leaves of countless trees, showing little interest in the grass at their feet. A little further, he saw shorter animals with round bodies and short legs and covered with thick white hide. They somewhat resembled pigs.

The sun slipped beyond the horizon, and it grew dark. The vehicle's light shone on the road ahead, illuminating Shenell's way. The ship's time was later, and though Diego had dozed on the shuttle, he was still tired. It was hard to keep his eyes open. He glanced at Rreengrol and saw that his friend appeared very relaxed. Fress's head rested against his side.

Above, the stars glittered like they did in the sky he saw from the pastures of his home planet. Then something sped across the sky. It was larger than the shooting stars he was used to, and it moved slower. The object glowed in a bright orange color, and then it changed to a deep yellow.

"What was that?"

"That's our master satellite, the one overseeing all of our smaller defensive satellites," Rreengrol murmured. "The satellites protect us from any enemies that might come from space, and they also monitor the weather."

"Oh."

"After we've had a good night's rest, I'll explain exactly what they do."

Diego chuckled. "The old grandfathers monitored the weather on my world. If their joints hurt, we knew a storm was coming, or it was going to turn cold. They knew the clouds, too. Such things as these satellites sound like they are much more accurate."

Rreengrol pulled on his whiskers. "I believe so, but to be honest, I've heard of such things among our ancestors."

A short time later, Shenell turned the vehicle up a narrower road between two tall fences. The road continued unchanged for a while until Diego saw a mound in the distance. By the lights flashing on at their approach, Diego saw it was a somewhat pointed building with three rows of windows. Shenell's vehicle stopped right in front, and they all slid out. Diego helped Rreengrol with the containers. Fress grabbed a smaller one, and they followed Rreengrol's mother up a short ramp. A door slid open to a well-lit room. Several loud voices called out what Diego recognized as a Grrlock greeting.

A small group of Grrlocks surrounded Rreengrol. Some of them were old, one appeared to be his age, and one younger. Diego guessed the one close to Rreengrol's age was his sister, and the younger one was his little brother. He noticed a table laden with a veritable fiesta and a banner hung from the ceiling with many greetings.

"A party," Fress said, still hanging on to her travel case.

"It has been a long time, young Commander Diego," Lershan explained to Diego and Fress, "since Rreengrol has visited us. Over two of our years. I have missed my mate's oldest."

Rreengrol's mother, or rather, stepmother, had a pelt longer than Rreengrol's, and it was also lighter, so light as to be cream colored, especially in front. Her tail was longer, with darker fur. "And your home?"

Diego gazed at her for a moment, thinking back to his own mother. "Rejas Hreeshan said I would never return home."

"Oh." Her green eyes widened, and her ears flicked. Despite her differences, Lershan reminded him of his mother. Her eyes showed understanding and concern for him, just as his mother would have done on occasions when she wasn't sick.

"The Seressin captured me."

Lershan growled softly in her throat. "Despicable practice."

"I miss my family, but I'm not a slave anymore. Rreengrol is my new brother." Diego watched Rreengrol continue his greetings to his brother and sister. "He is closer to me than my actual brother was." Still, Diego felt his throat close, and his eyes prickle with unshed tears. Despite all he had gained, he had lost so much.

He felt Lershan's soft arm pull him close. "Come with me, young Commander," Lershan said, guiding him to a door that slid open at their approach. A light came on, and the door shut behind them. The Grrlock mother pulled him over to a long bench that held them both. "You are yet a cub for all that you have saved ships and people. It is all right for you to grieve your losses." She purred as he cried against her shoulder.

Diego wasn't sure how long they were in the little room, but no one came after them, for which he was glad. He was fifteen and shouldn't be crying like a baby. Finally, Diego rubbed his hand across his eyes, took the handkerchief Lershan gave him, and blew his nose. Now, he was embarrassed. "I'm—I'm sorry, Señora Lershan."

"You have nothing whatsoever to be sorry for. There is much you have lost and much you have seen and had to deal with. And you are how old?"

Diego did some quick figuring. "I was fourteen Earth years when I was captured. So, I am fifteen now."

"Fifteen years old? Did you have a celebration? It seems

we need to have a party before you go back on board," she murmured.

"Oh, no. That's okay."

"Well," she pointed. "In that room is a place where you can wash up, and when you feel better, come and join us. We would like you to enjoy our hospitality. I know you are tired, so after the party, Rreengrol will show you and the Turengen — Fress? He will show you your rooms."

"Thank you, Señora."

She smiled as she got up. "What is this 'señora'?"

"You are married or mated to Rreengrol's father. In my culture, that woman is a señora. Your daughter is a señorita."

"What pretty titles. You must tell me more about your language while you are here." She laid her hand on top of his. "Everything will be all right, Diego. I can never thank you for the gift of having my son alive and back, even if for a little while."

She walked to the door. "Come on out when you're ready."

"Thank you." Diego strode toward the door Lershan indicated. It slid open for him, and a light turned on. He washed his face and neck, feeling much better, although he was still somewhat embarrassed by his emotional display.

After a while, he walked to the room serving as a sala, the great room.

Rreengrol greeted him. "Come, Diego, my brother-in-arms. You need to eat some of this wonderful food before my sister gobbles it down. The lighter-furred Grrlock cuffed him on the shoulder. "Diego, this unruly cub is Rrishan. Rrishan, this is Diego Perez."

"Welcome, and many thanks, Commander Diego Perez."

Diego smiled. "Just call me Diego."

"Oh, and Rreengrol, I am not a cub! I am as old as you were when you signed on to be a squire."

"I know."

The smallest cub was bouncing up and down. "Can I call

you Diego, too?"

"Of course."

"And this ball of fluff and energy is my little brother, Shegrol," Rreengrol added.

Diego met Shennell's parents, ate a little, and enjoyed watching everyone have a fun time. Fress stayed close to his side. Later, when he didn't think he could stay awake a moment longer and Fress was dozing, Rreengrol led them up the narrow ramp to the next level.

"You'll be sharing my room with me, and Fress, do you mind sharing my sister's room?"

"I can share with anyone. Grateful for a place to stay." She looked at Diego. "But shouldn't I be with you? To serve?"

"Not tonight, and we can talk about it tomorrow," Diego replied. When he stepped into Rreengrol's room, it was nothing like the cabin they had shared on Ziron's ship. This one was roomy, almost as large as Commander Ziron's quarters. The bed was also larger, easily fitting Diego's frame, which had grown some since his capture.

He pulled off his tunic, slid into the bed, and remembered nothing more.

CHAPTER SEVEN

Diego did not know what time of day it was when he woke up. There was no window to show the sun, and he couldn't see a clock either. Rreengrol was not in his bed, and Fress was sitting on the floor nearby, staring at him.

"Have you been here long?"

"Not long. Only twenty deca-cycles. About two hours."

"That certainly **is** long! And I bet you didn't have breakfast either."

"Sure, she did when Rrishan brought her something," Rreengrol said as he entered his room. "You slept hard. Recovered from your trip here?"

Diego sat up with a sigh. "Yes. Best night's sleep I've had in a long time." There were no dreams, nightmares, nothing but sound, restful sleep. "Fress, you are here to enjoy yourself, too. Yes, sometimes I will ask you for your help, but I am here to relax, and so are you."

Fress scratched her head. "Don't understand. Squires are supposed to serve."

"Yes, but I am ordering you to relax and have fun. I can't enjoy myself if I am watching you do stuff like a slave. You are a fellow warrior."

"Oh. Fellow warrior?"

"Well, a warrior in training, anyway."

Fress preened her pelt. "Yes. Warrior in training."

Diego laughed as he rose and stretched. "What are we doing today, my friend?" he asked Rreengrol.

"You said something about the beach."

"I don't want to put anyone out, Rreengrol."

"We'll go into the mountains after visiting Uncle Hrushan."

"All right, sounds good. What time is it?"

"Almost mid-meal."

"You're joking."

Rreengrol shook his head, then scratched behind his ear. "Get dressed. Mother is fixing mid-meal and some snacks for the trip. We'll come back after dark, but we still won't have much time if we don't get moving."

Diego went to shower and realized that instead of flowing water, it was more like a fog. Still, when he got out, he felt clean and wondered how a fog could do that. Throwing on one of his new outfits, Diego trotted down the ramp where Lershan greeted him. Rrishan and Shegrol were already sitting down.

"Rreengrol told me you slept well, Diego," Lershan said as she brought him a plate with what appeared to be a sandwich and several unknown condiments all around it.

Diego glanced at the others to see if there was a pre-meal custom. Apparently, there wasn't because Shegrol began eating his meal. With a soft growl from his mother, the cub slowed.

Diego's stomach gurgled, and he began. The food was delicious, and it didn't take long to finish.

"We will all be going to my brother Hrushan's denning, Diego. I hope you don't mind. It might be a little crowded in the vehicle," Lershan told him.

"That's okay. I am used to being crowded." Diego remembered his time when the large assault group crowded into a shuttle to save the Seressin commanders.

"Well, if you all will help me take these packages out, we'll go right away."

Soon, they were skimming along, driving past the

ranch lands, then through a pass in a mountain range. Almost immediately, Diego could see the sun glittering on a stretch of dark blue sand. The foam on top of the waves almost appeared golden. "Santa Maria!" Diego blurted. "That is much more beautiful than what I saw in the pictures."

"Yes, which is why Hrushan chose to live there, despite all the rain during the wet season," Lershan explained.

"How bad is the rainy season?" Diego asked.

"It averages about a quarter of our year."

"But to have this the rest of the time," he mused.

"Indeed," Rreengrol's mother said. She drove along a road paralleling the shoreline. Then she turned into a space just below what looked like a cave with a portion of a house built over the entrance. There were many such dwellings. As soon as Lershan stopped their vehicle, an exceptionally large Grrlock walked to the railing. He waved and called out as the group slid out of the transport.

"That is my brother," Lershan informed them.

Fress stared at Rreengrol's uncle before pattering up the path leading to the wooden porch. Diego stood back as the family greeted each other.

"Uncle, this is my friend, Diego, sub-commander to Marix Ziron. This is Squire Fress."

"Welcome, welcome!" Hrushan boomed, almost drowning the sound of the surf on the beach. "Come inside my humble den."

While Rreengrol's house was rather spacious, this den was a fraction of the size. Diego glanced around in the dimly lit home. There seemed to be a main room with the dining and cooking area and another room that probably functioned as a bedroom. Diego stood since there were not enough chairs.

"I am such a poor host. Sister, sit on my couch. Cubs, I have swept my floor. Pull up a piece of it," Hrushan said with a yowling laugh.

Diego sat down next to Rreengrol and Rrishan while Fress sat next to him. He had learned during the last year not to feel insulted over being considered a child.

Hrushan gazed at Diego. "Forgive me. I guess I shouldn't be calling you and Rreengrol children, having been in battle."

"I don't mind," Diego said quickly. Rreengrol nodded.

"We don't get many details of such things here. It must have been harrowing," Hrushan said. "Can you tell me about it?"

"A little later, brother. They came to enjoy the beach."

"Ah, of course, of course. You have fun in the water. If you catch anything, make sure you hang on to it so I can cook it for dinner." Again, the booming laugh.

"And watch Shegrol!" Lershan called after them.

Diego, Fress, Rreengrol, and his siblings all dashed down the path, across the road, and down the blue sands to the water. Even through his shoes, Diego could feel the warmth of the sand. He stooped and picked up a handful, letting it flow through his fingers. When the sun hit the particles in his hand, it reflected painfully into his eyes. Diego gazed toward the horizon.

"Were there beaches like this on your home world?" Rrishan asked.

"Yes, near to my father's hacienda," Diego replied.

"No wonder you wanted to visit," she added. "Did you learn how to swim?"

Diego shook his head. "We only occasionally visited the beaches near my home and only when my mother insisted. She came from the Indies where they had many beaches, and she loved the warm Caribbean waters." He wondered why he was saying all of this to Rreengrol's sister. He hadn't even mentioned this to his friend. "Of course, the Pacific wasn't always that warm."

"This time of year, the water here is very warm," Rrishan explained. "Shall we see if the streeshin come to nibble on our toes?"

"Streeshin?"

"They are little fish that make good bait for the big fish living further out."

"Oh. How do you catch them?" Diego didn't see any nets.

"With our claws." She showed her feet with her shoes off, unsheathing the claws.

With a laugh, Diego pulled off his walking shoes, which he didn't want to get wet. He laid them well out of reach of the surf. Then he wiggled his toes. "No claws."

"You let them nibble; I will catch them."

"Wouldn't a net be easier?"

"I guess for you," Rreengrol interjected. "But for us, it's a matter of coordination and skill. I bet Uncle Hrushan has a net. He's not patient enough to use his claws."

"Oh, okay. I'll be right back." Shegrol splashed as the water surged over his feet. "Do you want me to find something for you to make a castle out of sand?" Diego asked the cub. "A shovel or something?"

"Castle?"

Diego nodded.

"How do you make a castle? What is a castle?"

Diego laughed. "An old-fashioned type of house—uh, denning."

"Sure! I'd like to do that."

"I'll see what I can find."

Diego ran up the path to Hrushan's house but paused when he reached the door. Lershan and her brother were deep in conversation, and he hated to disturb them.

"I don't understand the government at all!" Hrushan growled. "They gripe about the Seressin Empire, but I bet they'd be howling equally loud if they didn't have Seressin advanced technology. I just wish I knew if the Seressins are changing a few of their more repugnant ideologies—like slavery. Why do they continue that foul practice? Aren't there enough volunteers to man their starships?"

Lershan sighed. "Rreengrol's ship...."

"*Star Devourer*?" Hrushan interrupted.

"Yes. The commander's squire was a slave, captured from a backward, pre-industrial world about a year ago."

"He must have shown great promise. Still, Diego had to be scared to death if he wasn't familiar with technology."

"He earned his freedom in half a year by saving Ziron's life. Rreengrol's, too. As much as I despise that reprehensible custom, I am grateful Diego was around," Lershan replied.

"But if the Seressin aren't willing to listen to their member worlds, they might just have a revolution on their hands. That would be disastrous with the Resh still trying to weaken the Seressin Empire."

"I can't help but agree with you. I think Commander Hreeshan is going to speak to the Assembly in a few cycles. Oh, and the empire is looking at women in warrior roles. Rrishan is applying."

"Doesn't that frighten you, Lershan? I hope Hreeshan can make an impression. I wish he could talk some sense into those hard-skulled reptiles."

Diego decided not to interrupt the discussion, even though he wanted to. He looked around the veranda, then below it. That's where he found some tools he could use—something like a short-handled shovel, a bucket, and a smaller container. As he turned to leave, Diego saw a small net. He carried everything back down to the beach.

CHAPTER EIGHT

Diego put the conversation out of his mind as he showed Shegrol how to build a castle. The sand was almost too coarse, but the cub solved the problem. He made something like his own house. It was pyramid-shaped, with a road, a few windows, and a small door rimmed with twigs.

After a while, Diego left Shegrol and joined the others. Rreengrol had a sack with a few of the streeshin flopping around inside. "Just stand quietly in the water up to your ankles."

Diego did as he was told. He saw dark little shapes swimming around out of reach of his net. Several came closer but darted away before he could think of lowering his net.

Finally, Rreengrol laughed and called him back on the beach. "I don't think they like how you taste!"

"They didn't get close enough to find out."

Rreengrol laughed again. "They didn't like your bare legs. It scared them away."

"Ha ha!"

"Doesn't matter. We have enough to bait our hooks and catch some actual fish." Rreengrol pointed to four poles. That was the only similarity to fishing poles he had seen before his capture. These poles had a line coming out of the tip, and there were devices on the grip end. Rreengrol showed him how to bait the hook.

Diego studied the little streeshin they were using as bait.

They looked a lot like miniature snakes with fins, bright blue green with black and yellow stripes running along their sinuous bodies. The teeth were tiny.

Rreengrol showed him how the device on the handle worked. Diego watched the demonstration. It was like flicking a whip. When Rreengrol swung the pole, the line came out and shot into the water at least thirty feet away.

The first time Diego swung his pole, the line only came out a little, the end dropping at his feet.

"A little more force, my friend."

Diego had more success the next time he swung it. The hook and bait sank into the waves, leaving him uncertain of his next move.

"Push this button." Rrishan showed him a little yellow button. "And your line will pull back in. Let go of the button, and it will stop."

Diego enjoyed this new way of fishing and hoped he would catch something. A shout from Shegrol brought his attention away from the ocean to the cub who had joined in the fishing. He was struggling to pull in a large fish. Rreengrol came to his rescue. They extricated the fish from the hook and tossed it in a large container with a lid.

Diego saw what appeared to be stumpy legs behind the front and back fins. The body was quite large around, almost barrel shaped. Then, a tug on his own line almost jerked the pole from his hands. His fish pulled away from the shore, and Diego tried to reel him in.

"Use the button a little at a time," Rrishan called.

Diego tried, but the fish pulled more out than the young man could pull in. He backed away from the shore as he tried to use the button. Finally, the fish stopped struggling a little, and Diego drew the line in. He drew it in some more, and Rreengrol used a long pole with a hook to drag it onto the beach. It wasn't the same kind of fish as Shegrol's. This one had huge fins in front and a tail half the size of the rest of the body, which was flat. It would feed several of them.

Rreengrol lugged the fish over to the second container and shoved it in. "Nice job for a first catch."

"Thanks."

They continued fishing for a while longer until each of them caught a fish large enough to cook.

Rrishan talked Fress into using Shegrol's pole to catch a fish. "Better to just jump in and chase a fish," the Turengen commented.

"Except most of them would chase you. The farther out you go, the bigger they get," Rrishan explained.

They lugged the containers and fishing equipment up the hill. As they reached Hrushan's denning, Diego thought again of the conversation between the two Grrlocks. He was uncomfortable saying anything and admitting he eavesdropped. He would talk to Rreengrol alone, but the opportunity didn't come that day. First, there was the task of cleaning the fish and then helping Hrushan and Lershan cook them. After dinner, they sat on the terrace and watched the sunset, then they drove back to Rreengrol's denning. Shegrol fell asleep against Diego's shoulder, and he didn't want to wake the cub. Rreengrol couldn't stop yawning by the time they reached the house. Both went to bed almost immediately.

CHAPTER NINE

"Are you eager to get away into the mountains?" Rreengrol asked.

"Yes. They look much like the mountains to the east of my father's rancho. Are we all going?"

"You, me, Rrishan, and Fress. It will be rugged but worth it."

"When are we going?"

"Tomorrow. We'll get ready today, and Father will take us to the beginning of the trail. You and Fress will have to get the orientation since you've never been up there."

"Is it dangerous?"

"After what we've been through?"

Diego laughed. "You have a point. Just tell me what we need to do to prepare."

"You came with most of what we need. Any other supplies we don't have here, we'll pick up on the way tomorrow."

It was a pleasant day. Shegrol was jealous he couldn't go and whined about it. He watched the preparations but didn't interfere.

Diego found the pack he had purchased on the ship to be incredibly light but roomy. At Rreengrol's suggestion, he packed the smaller weaponry he had brought with him, the survival equipment, and rations. The clothing Rreengrol helped him pick out folded compactly and allowed him to get it all into the pack along with other items the others thought he needed.

Just before the last meal, Rreengrol pulled out a map. It was printed on something durable, like the ones Diego was familiar with, rather than what he viewed on a computer.

"We are going up this mountain." Rreengrol pointed to a particular spot. "We'll camp at the bottom the first night, get the orientation, and then camp a quarter of the way up the second night. Hopefully, we'll make another quarter of the distance on the third night and reach close to the summit on the fourth night."

"Why so long, Rreengrol?" Rrishan asked. "We've done it in less time."

"Because we have two people in the group who haven't climbed mountains any time in the recent past. *I* haven't climbed in the recent past!" Rreengrol wiggled his whiskers and smiled to show he wasn't angry. "Besides, I want to enjoy the mountain wildlife."

"To look at them or eat them? Are you thinking we'll meet one of our mountain cousins?" Rrishan teased.

"Don't be silly. If there are any left, they won't be coming to greet us."

"Mountain cousins?" Fress asked before Diego could say anything.

"We were already a people who were exploring various technologies and living in communities when the Seressin contacted us...."

"Took some of our people," Rrishan interjected.

"That was a long time ago. They discovered we were better allies than slaves." Rreengrol gave her a warning glance.

"Is that how the Seressins begin all alliances?"

"Not anymore, Diego," Rreengrol explained. "The Seressin government studies the worlds they find through exploration or accident, and if they are advanced enough, they will negotiate with them."

"Apparently, they didn't consider my world advanced

enough."

"By your own admission, you said your transportation was on top of animals or wind-powered water vessels, and your most advanced weapons were concussion projectiles."

"Regardless of how well I have advanced in Seressin society, the taking of slaves is still wrong!" Diego snapped.

"I agree, but I think that is changing, even if it's a slow change."

"My people can apply to become squires now," Fress reminded them. "They couldn't before!"

"But what about these mountain cousins?" Diego reminded his friends.

"Oh, there used to be a group of Grrlocks who lived as our ancestors did without technology. Some of them were larger than us, taller and stronger."

Diego thought about how agile and strong Hreeshan was and figured he didn't want to meet one of these cousins. "Used to be?"

"None have been seen for several generations," Rreengrol explained.

"So, you think they all died out?" Diego asked.

Rreengrol nodded. "Occasionally, someone claims to have found something, but no one can prove it."

"Oh."

Lershan interrupted the discussion with a call to dinner.

Diego again remembered the conversation he had overheard the day before and his determination to talk to Rreengrol privately, maybe before bed.

Shennel monopolized dinner, giving them advice, and Lershan asking Rrishan if she had this or that necessary item. Diego had never had such attention in his family and was jealous.

Later in the bedroom, with everything packed and their gear by the door to take down first thing in the morning, Diego lay on his bed. He considered the conversation at Uncle Hrushan's denning. "Rreengrol?"

"Mmm?" Rreengrol was lying on his bed, apparently ready to sleep.

Still, Diego wanted to know the prevailing feelings about the Seressin. "Can I ask you a question?"

"Sure," came the mumbled response.

"Uh, Rreengrol?"

"Mmph."

"Tomorrow."

"Tomorrow what?"

"Never mind. Sleep well."

"You, too. Going to be early...."

With that, the Grrlock was asleep. Diego wished he could do that. Rreengrol had always been that way, but when needful, he could wake and be ready for action in a few heartbeats, something Diego still had problems with. This time, though, he fell asleep quickly, and there were no dreams.

"Wake up!" A large Grrlock was standing over him—the largest Grrlock he had ever seen. It grimaced, and Diego saw huge teeth.

"Wake up!" the voice called again, but this time it was Rreengrol's voice.

When Diego opened his eyes to the bright overhead light, he saw Rreengrol and Fress dressed and ready for the day.

"If you don't hurry and dress, you'll miss my mother's marvelous send-off first meal."

With a groan, Diego sat up and stretched. "I'll be ready shortly. Go on down."

Rreengrol cuffed him on the shoulder and laughed. "I still say you'd better hurry. Rrishan can eat her weight in fish cakes and fast bread."

"Okay. Okay!" Diego slid out of bed. Fress hesitated by the door. "Get breakfast, Fress. You don't have to wait for me."

She ran a hand through her whiskers, then turned and

dashed down the ramp to the dining room. Diego showered and dressed in the travel clothes he had picked out the night before. They were lightweight but would protect him in rain or to a certain degree of cold. When he headed out of the room, he was embarrassed to see someone had taken his pack.

CHAPTER TEN

Diego stood in awe at the surrounding scenery. The place where Rreengrol's father had left them, what Rreengrol called a trailhead, made him think of the mountains of his home planet. These mountains were much taller.

"We're climbing that one tomorrow." Rrishan pointed toward the tallest peak.

"I think climbing is the correct word for it," Diego said with a wry grin. "Because I don't think we'll be hiking."

Rreengrol laughed. "There are plenty of well-defined trails, and they don't all go straight up. We'll see how good our training has been."

"And if I keep up with you two, then I should be capable of applying to be a squire," Rrishan exclaimed.

"I think you are capable already," Fress quipped.

"Thanks, Fress."

Diego examined the area Rreengrol and Rrishan chose for them to spend the first night. There were many trees with thick growing brush. He could see other campsites, but the foliage made each one private.

Diego helped Rreengrol and Rrishan set up two pyramid-shaped tents. The poles holding up the lightweight but tough material snapped into place with little effort. Diego and Fress laid the material across the frame and staked it down.

Once Diego had helped the vaqueros raise a shelter. It was

a lean-to they erected when they gathered the cattle from the hills during a time of the rains. Normally, in California, the men slept in the open when they were too far away from the hacienda to return home at night. Diego wondered if it rained a lot on Grrlock to require this kind of shelter. He had seen no rain yet.

Rrishan and Fress would sleep in one, and he and Rreengrol would sleep in the other one. There was enough room in the tents to lay out their sleeping gear and store their packs. At first, Diego gazed at the material just above his face and felt a little closed in, but hearing the noises of the forest and the murmur of Grrlock voices in the distance eased his anxiety.

Despite that, he didn't stay in the tent any longer than he had to. Rreengrol, who was setting up a small cooking apparatus, gazed at him. "Are you all right? Is the tent all right?"

"I just have to get used to it," Diego admitted.

"What did you use on your home world?"

"A bed," he said with a smile. Then he explained his excursions with the vaqueros.

"You weren't worried about wild animals or rain?"

"We had a fire to scare off animals. If there were a lot of dangerous animals where we were, one of us would stand guard." Diego studied the tents. "How do those fend off wild animals?"

"There is a repeller in the poles to make the tent undesirable to any wild animal. We will be protected out in the wild. At least while we're sleeping."

Diego pointed at the apparatus Rreengrol had set up. "And I assume that will heat any food we brought?"

Rreengrol nodded. "And have some of Lershan's good cooking for tonight."

"I'm going to the water and swim," Fress announced. "After we do our orientation."

"It'll be a little cold."

"Not a problem for me. My pelt repels water. And a layer

of fat under the skin that protects us."

"I'll go with you," Diego said.

"Me, too," Rrishan added.

"I will watch our campground."

"So, you have some deviant citizens, too?" Diego teased.

"A few."

"What my brother really wants to do is take a nap," Rrishan smirked.

"Fighting Resh is hard work." Rreengrol grinned.

Diego laughed. "That was a long time ago! But enjoy your nap."

The three followed a well-trod path winding past other camping spaces. About half of them were occupied. The trio got some extra-long gazes from the Grrlocks, watching them pass by. One stopped them.

"I recognize the Turengen," an older Grrlock with a white-tipped pelt said to Rrishan. "But not the other."

Diego found it disconcerting having someone talk about you right in front of your face.

It disturbed Rrishan as well. "My *friend* is a sub...."

Diego put his hand on Rrishan's arm. He didn't feel this was the time or place to pull rank. "I am a human from a mid-sized planet far from the Seressin core," he said politely in the Grrlock language.

"Never heard of humans. Obviously, mammalian."

"Yes, sir."

"You'll have to come by and tell me about your planet," the Grrlock said.

"If I can, but we will not be here long."

"Ah, you are here to test yourselves on the mountain?"

Diego nodded.

"Good luck to you."

"Thank you, sir." They went on, getting more stares, but no one else stopped them. Soon, they reached a large-sized stream.

Diego would have classified it as a small river. The crystal blue water splashed against rocks and flowed into deeper areas where they couldn't see the bottom.

Fress eyed the river hungrily, then sighed. "Let us go to the orientation." She and Diego walked down the path to a building that had a roof but no walls. The breeze refreshed him as an older Grrlock told them about safety on the mountain trails. Rreengrol's father told them the same thing on the drive to the trailhead, so Diego was grateful the orientation was short.

Soon, they were back at the river. Fress pulled off her jumpsuit and dived in. In the shallower waters, she swam as fast as a bullet. In a deeper spot, she leaped out of the water and then splashed back in.

Diego pulled off his boots and socks, and rolled up the bottoms of his pants, then sat on the bank with his feet dangling in the water. He almost jerked them up; the water was so cold.

Rrishan laughed. She sat on a higher bank, not letting her boots touch the water. "This time of the year is not the best time to swim. Unless you're a Turengen, I guess."

Diego laughed with her but kept his feet in the frigid water.

"What are you doing with these Seressin slaves, cub? Didn't your sire teach you any better?"

Diego jerked around. A tall, dark-furred Grrlock with crystal blue eyes stared at Rrishan. She jumped up and glared at him. "My sire tutored my brother and me to serve with honor. Besides, they are not slaves!"

Diego climbed up on the bank. He felt awkward without his footwear, but he drew himself up as tall as he could. Anger was replacing his shock. "May I ask who you are?"

"You may not. I do not talk to mrees except to give them orders. Why the import/export consul allows vermin to pollute our planet, I'll never be able to figure."

A small splash told Diego Fress was watching as well.

"There are many pollutants, señor. Just for your

information, I am Sub-Commander, mid-class Diego Perez, personal squire to Commander Ziron. I earned my rank and my freedom with dedication and hard work. Your insults are uncalled for."

The Grrlock didn't flinch. Only his whiskers twitched. "A freed slave to fawn over a Seressin butcher. You're still not welcome here."

Diego looked behind the Grrlock. "Where is the rest of the Grrlock population that feels the way you do?"

Other Grrlocks fishing downstream glared at them, but Diego couldn't tell if it was because they sympathized with the tall Grrlock or because they disturbed their fishing.

"Who are you?" Rrishan demanded.

"Waugh!" As suddenly as the Grrlock had appeared, he disappeared, stomping down a path along the stream. The other Grrlocks went back to their fishing.

"I'm sorry, Diego — Fress."

"You have nothing to be sorry for, Rrishan. Do you have any idea what brought that on?" Diego remembered the conversation between Rrishan's mother and uncle and wondered about the political climate here. Politics grew sometimes heated back in California, but he ignored it.

"Done swimming. It's time to go back," Fress said, shaking the water droplets off her pelt. She grabbed her jumpsuit and trotted back to their camp.

"I'm not sure, Diego. I guess I don't pay as much attention to the news as I should. I know some Grrlocks would prefer not to be allied to the Seressin. Rreengrol might have a better understanding of all this."

"He's not been on your planet for a long while."

She shrugged, and Diego dropped the topic for the moment. He could hear the low growl in her throat. They walked back in silence. Rreengrol had the cooker working and their dinners warming on top, but he watched them as they returned to their camping space.

"Fress tells me you met one of the dissidents."

"Is that what they are called?" Diego asked.

Rreengrol nodded.

"If you mean rude and nasty, then I guess we did," Diego answered with a tight smile. "Are these dissidents common on Grrlock?"

"No. They are a very vocal minority. I'm sorry one of them showed up on our vacation. While most Grrlocks don't have any reason to interact with Seressin, they also don't mind them."

Diego sat on a log. "Such exists on all worlds, I am afraid." He told Rreengrol about the conversation between his friend's dam and his uncle.

Rreengrol sighed. "I guess the anti-Seressin dissidents are more vocal than they used to be. Thing is, we've gotten used to having allies, and the Seressin are the most powerful. I can't help but wonder who would have stepped in if the Seressin weren't here?"

"The Resh?"

"Yeah, I guess. Although that possibility makes me want to gag."

Diego smiled. It would make him gag, too.

"Until the last couple of generations, a non-reptilian couldn't hope to be a full commander."

"Commander Hreeshan and Commander Weelix?"

"Hreeshan is one of the first, and Marix Ziron fought for his rise in rank. Weelix received his full commander rank recently." Rreengrol pulled on his boots. "I want to command a ship someday."

"I believe you will, my friend."

"It's still hard, Diego."

"I know."

CHAPTER ELEVEN

Despite feeling a bit crowded in the small tent, Diego fell asleep quickly and slept soundly all night. The large Grrlock appeared once in his dream but didn't speak and did nothing except stare at him. It woke him up as the sun was rising over the eastern hills. When he realized he had only been dreaming, Diego relaxed and listened to the songs of several birds in the tree limbs above them. They sounded a little like the birds of his homeland, except they were louder.

"Awake and ready to go?" Rreengrol mumbled from under his covers.

"Yes, I guess so." He declined to say anything about the Grrlock in his dream. "I'll be right back." Pulling on his clothes and boots, Diego crawled out and stretched. Then, he walked down to the public bathroom. He did his business, washed up, then returned to the camp. Diego received only curious looks from other early risers.

When he returned to their campground, Diego studied a pit surrounded by large, flat-topped rocks, which Diego knew was for a fire. He gathered up dead wood and laid it over some shredded paper. With a striker, he started a modest fire. He laid a rack across the pit and dug out some of the preserved meat that reminded him of salted beef. With the leftover food Lershan packed away for them, he figured they would have a hearty, as well as a warm breakfast.

About the time the food was ready, Rreengrol poked his head out of the tent. "So, you are a chef, along with all your other talents," he said with a grin.

"No, but sometimes I oversaw getting the morning fire started for the vaqueros when we were out in the hills. And sometimes I also helped cook."

"Smells good. I'll be right out."

"So will we," Rrishan's muffled voice sounded inside the other tent.

It was every bit as good as the meals Lershan had cooked at Rreengrol's home. Rrishan took down the tents with Fress's help and packed them, along with their equipment. Within an hour, they were ready for the first day of their climb.

Insects joined the birds singing, their trills adding depth to the woodland chorus. As Diego settled the large pack on his back, he gazed at the mountain they were planning to climb. It seemed to go straight up. He had heard tales of mountains in South America like this one, but at the time, he hadn't believed the stories.

"The trail weaves partly around the mountain. It may be steep at times, but not the entire distance," Rreengrol said, shouldering his own pack. "By the way, we'll be going high enough that I included a re-breather mask in each pack. If you feel oxygen-deprived, let me know, and I'll help you get it on."

"Thanks."

At first, Rrishan was eager to point out the birds, various rock formations, flowers, and shrubs. Diego found them fascinating. They were also like what was on his world. Most of the birds had plumage, allowing them to blend in with the trees and rocks — gray and brown, with some spots of color on their tails or breasts. The flowers, though, seemed to make up for the birds' lack. Along the trail were large red and purple flowers. From inside those, liquid dripped on the ground. Where the nectar dripped, insects gathered, some climbing up the stems to drink right from the source.

"Don't mess with those flowers. That nectar may be wonderful to the insects but is poison to us. The brighter the flowers, the more toxic they are."

"Really? That's interesting."

As they walked further, the foliage changed. The plants were shorter, while the trees seemed to be taller and spindlier. Diego saw hikers going up, but none returning. He asked Rrishan about it.

"There's another trail leading down from the summit."

"Oh. What happens if someone gets part way up and has to come down?"

She giggled. "You ready to leave?"

"No, but sometimes, don't people get sick or hurt up here?"

"Yes, it happens. There are paths that cut over to the downward trail. Just like there are areas to camp and rest."

Halfway through the day, they stopped at a wide area with several tables and a view of mountains. Below, sparkling streams flowed through narrow valleys. Clouds shrouded a few distant mountains. A breeze swirled down the trail. As they continued, it strengthened into a full-fledged wind.

"You also have a pair of protective lenses in your pack if the wind gets too strong," Rreengrol reminded them.

"I may need them soon." Diego wiped his watering eyes. The sun still shone, but he noticed clouds building closer to their mountain. His lenses were hanging from his pack, and he got them out while walking. "Looks like we might have a storm before the day is out, too."

"Might," his friend said.

"Will," Fress said.

"How can you tell?" Rrishan asked.

"Ears pop. Whiskers feel heavy."

"Your whiskers feel heavy?"

She shrugged. "It just is. We understand our bodies when they tell us things."

"I think the Seressin commanders have totally underestimated your people," Diego commented.

"Your people, too," Fress replied.

"I'm the only one."

"I know. If they had known what you could do, they would have taken more of you."

Diego stopped short. "What did I do?"

Rreengrol snorted. "Your honor is part of your life, not something you memorize from one of Anaar's lessons. I think even the commander picked up on that."

Diego blushed. "I'm not the only one."

"No, I know that. Right time and right place. Plus, you seemed very susceptible to the influences of the foretelling dreams," Rreengrol pointed out. "Do other humans have that talent? Is it common on your planet?"

Diego shook his head. "I didn't even have that talent before my capture. I have wondered how it came about."

"Maybe being around other beings, eating other food, being in space," Fress ventured with a shrug of her shoulders. "Who knows? It happened and seems to happen when needed."

"I guess."

As they continued, the wind grew so strong their words were carried away like dust, and the conversation ended. Diego walked, leaning forward. One gust threatened to knock him off the path.

"This...not forecast!" Rreengrol shouted.

"Need to find shelter," Diego practically screamed. There was no rain yet, but the clouds were lowering, and they'd soon not be able to see the path. He saw the swaying shapes of a stand of trees, and he grabbed Rreengrol's sleeve. Diego pointed, and they all made their way to what he hoped was safety.

A medium-trunked tree seemed to be the anchor for a

half-dozen younger trees.

"Find a space between the trunks!" Rreengrol shouted. "Get out your all-weather jackets. When the winds slacken, we can get out the tents."

Diego pulled off his pack and hunkered down between two younger trees. He pulled the lightweight jacket out of his pack and put it on. Fress crawled into his lap. She already had her jacket on. Diego didn't protest. What she did would help them both.

A touch on his shoulder told Diego that Rreengrol was behind him. He glanced around and barely made out Rrishan in the deepening gloom, sitting next to her brother. The wind was howling through the limbs above them. Diego hoped none of them broke. An explosive blast of thunder above them rattled his teeth. Lightning flashed, and then a deluge of rain followed. Diego hunched over Fress.

The limbs only partially protected them from the rain. It drummed down on them with the ferocity of bullets, and Diego felt himself slipping into semi-consciousness. For a few moments, he found it hard to draw breath. Then the storm eased up—the rain, first, and then the wind. Finally, the wind stopped, and the rain became a drizzle.

"Tents!" Rreengrol called out, and they pulled the parts out of their packs and began putting the tents together just outside the stand of trees.

"Still going to be wet," Diego pointed out.

"Watch," Rrishan said. When they finished, she pulled identical devices out from his pack and attached them inside the two tents. Then she pushed a button on each one and stepped back. There was a whirring noise, loud at first, then it softened and finally quit. Rrishan ducked into her tent, and Fress followed on her heels.

Diego peered into his and Rreengrol's tent and saw that it was bone dry. His friend pulled out the device, opened it up, and let the water pour out. Then he stuffed it back into the pack.

"Dehumidifier."

"Whatever it is, it worked," Diego said. With no reservations, he crawled into the tent and took off his jacket. Surprisingly, no water seeped through the fabric. Rreengrol pushed in his pack, then Diego's. He crawled in after them.

"No warmed-up food tonight," the Grrlock said.

CHAPTER TWELVE

It rained intermittently through the night. The wind blew a symphony that would have made it impossible to hear a wolf or a mountain lion if such lived on this world. Still, Diego fell asleep.

He woke up in an opulently decorated audience room that made the one on Commander Ziron's ship look shabby. He wore his squire's uniform, but it was torn in places and dusty. He had been on a mountain with his friends. How did he get to a different place – in his uniform – in that state? Next to him on one side were Rrishan and Fress, bound in chains. Why? Where were they? His thoughts shot through his mind like bullets. Why wasn't he in chains? In front of him were several raised seats, and on them sat three Resh, dressed as rulers would be. The one in the middle appeared to be in charge. His mottled skin was darker, and he was bigger, more bloated. How Diego wished he had some kind of weapon, even an anfrees or a sword.

Not only were these Resh ornate, but their surroundings were lavish as well. They wore silken garments encrusted with jewels and adorned with tons of fancy needlework. They spoke in their own croaking language, but he understood them. Why?

"Regardless that you did what we requested and that you and your comrades accomplished what we wanted," the middle and larger Resh began. "Your life was forfeit from the beginning. You will die for what you did to our empire. For destroying our ships and warriors."

Diego was confused, feeling he had missed the first part of this drama or dream.

"Yes, you have come out of a drug fog," the one on the left explained. He was laughing. "Good timing."

"Show them. Show them how the Resh are superior. Show this mammalian vermin he would have been better off allying with us than with the blustering Seressin."

The one on the right pointed to a blank wall, and Diego turned to look. The scene showed the Seressin supreme commander's ship, specifically an exceptionally large room called the Hall of Heroes, which was the main audience hall for the Supreme Commander to greet dignitaries. Supreme Commander Marzor left the room and entered a large shuttle with a retinue of a dozen Seressin guards and other officials. The shuttle took off and flew a short distance to Commander Ziron's ship. After docking, the supreme commander and his group made their way to the **Star Devourer's** audience hall. Soon, he was sitting in a large seat that Marix Ziron would sit in. Marix Ziron stood next to Marzor.

A large contingent of the ship's compliment greeted the leader of all Seressin's worlds, and then the sub-commanders and squires left. Instead of leaving, Diego and the two Grrlocks pulled out small weapons and killed all the Seressin left in the room. They ran from the room, down several corridors. Guards shot and killed Rreengrol and then Hreeshan, but Diego avoided the fire and made it to a shuttle. He took off into space, blasted the one ship opposing him, and made it away from the Seressin ships.

Rrishan turned to him. Fress just looked stricken.

Diego didn't remember doing any of this. What had happened? Why did he do it?

"And to think I wanted to be a squire like you and my brother!" Rrishan spat.

She was bathed in a glow. When it disappeared, so had she. Fress only looked at Diego with large eyes filled with confusion. Then she, too, disappeared. Diego turned back to the bloated Resh on their thrones as one of them fired a weapon at him. He saw the glow, and then he saw darkness — the inside of the tent.

A dream! Diego sucked in a deep breath. What did it mean? Was this a foretelling dream? It had to be! Fress and Rrishan had been with him. Rreengrol and Hreeshan were with him on the *Star Devourer*. The people in his dream, all but Hreeshan, were with him now. Something was going to happen soon.

"Rreengrol!" he called out in the darkness. A soft light at the top of the tent responded to his voice.

His friend's soft growl was the only other sound.

"Rreengrol! Wake up!"

"What has you awake and in a panic this time of night?" he grumbled.

"Something's going to happen. I had a dream. The Resh...."

Then something happened. The tent fell on top of them, squashing them to the ground. A shout from the other tent. Clatter and grunting voices above them. Something hissed. Then there was nothing.

CHAPTER THIRTEEN

Diego woke to shadows, but he couldn't figure out where he was. It wasn't the tent because he was sitting against a smooth wall. He remembered the grunting voices before he lost consciousness. Where had he heard those voices before? He saw three dark mounds in the room with him, one smaller than the other two. Fress? He leaned over and touched the closest mound. There was a groan.

"Fress?" he whispered. "Are you all right?"

Diego's head pounded as he moved. He stifled his own moan as the pounding reached into his eyes. He tried to think back to their capture.

The pounding in his head kept him from thinking deeply. He slid over, reached out, and felt Fress again. This time, she didn't move. Keeping one hand on the wall, Diego shuffled in the other direction. He felt Rreengrol and then Rrishan. Both were alive. Diego did not know where they were and how they got here.

But he knew, at least a little. He had seen another foretelling dream, and now he had to figure out what to do to change this one, too. The headache made it hard to think, but he had to!

Then the door slid open, the light beyond blinding him. Diego threw his hand in front of his eyes. Someone grabbed him and jerked him out of the cell. The door slid shut. He stumbled and almost fell.

"Walk!" a gravelly voice barked. It sounded like a croak.

Resh! A wave of nausea passed through his body, but he could squelch it—barely. "Why?" he began.

"Shut up!" The squat, bumpy-skinned creature jerked him again.

By this time, Diego could see, and he kept up with the Resh guard. He also kept quiet. He would find out what they wanted soon enough. Diego tried to observe as much as he could without making his head and stomach hurt worse.

They continued down the corridor and then entered an elevator. Soon, the door opened again. The Resh pushed him into a room like the meeting room Commander Ziron used to confer with his commanders and sub-commanders. There were several Resh sitting together behind a large table. Their enormous mouths opened wide in croaking laughter. To one side sat several Grrlocks. One of them was the one who had been so obnoxious at the mountain base.

Even vacations were dangerous, he thought. It didn't look like he was going to make it to his sixteenth birthday.

The Resh talked among themselves. Diego did not know what they were saying despite what he had heard in his dream. He found he had an aptitude for languages but never felt the need to learn more of the Resh language. Now, he wished he had.

There was nothing else to do except wait. Living with the Seressin had taught him patience. Diego remembered the dream, trying to pull up every detail. These Resh looked much like the ones in the dream, but they were not as ornately dressed. Also, as in the dream, the one in the middle was bigger and darker.

"You do not have your precious Commander Ziron now, mrees," the Resh in the middle spoke to him in Seressin.

Diego bristled at the slave term, but he would say nothing, not yet.

"We could execute your sentence right now, mrees, but we are a fair and generous race. Perhaps there is a way to commute your sentence."

"What sentence?" Diego asked, too curious to keep quiet.

The one on the right spoke this time. "You were sentenced to death for your crimes against the Resh Empire."

"Oh." Diego paused. He figured he knew the answer to the next question. "What way are you talking about?"

The middle Resh leaned forward, his bulbous eyes eager. "Do a slight task for us, and we'll let you live."

"Live?" Diego took a deep breath. "Live?" He might put his foot squarely into a cow patty with this, but he couldn't seem too eager. "I am a sub-commander with position and some wealth. How would you propose I live—you called me a mrees?" Diego forced a laugh. "Whatever the job is, your reward isn't enough. No, thanks. You might as well line me up against the wall now." He glared at the Resh.

The Resh croaked among themselves, occasionally turning to scowl at him. If Diego was correctly guessing what they wanted him to do, then he figured no one else could get as close to Commander Ziron as he could. Of course, he might also overstate his importance. He remembered his dream included Commander Hreeshan and Rreengrol, as well as them having some kind of mind-controlling drug or device.

"You presume much," said the Resh on the right. "You are in no position to make demands."

"You just said you were going to kill me. I'm just saying...."

"No wonder you succeeded at that battle. You have a great deal of nerve," said the one in the middle.

Diego scowled. He figured he'd better keep still and see what they decided.

"If you do this job, and you do it well, we could use someone of your skills among our military. We would match your rank. You will have a handsome salary and a bounty for your victory," the middle Resh announced.

Diego knew that was a lie, but he still had to get away and

figure out a way to change the dream. "What do you want me to do?"

"You will return to your ship and kill Commander Ziron and the Supreme Commander he will be entertaining."

Diego remembered the dream, but when they said what the plot was, he was still stunned. He didn't have to act surprised. "That would be impossible! Do you realize what kind of security there'd be with the Supreme Commander on board?"

The Resh on the left croaked out something Diego didn't think was very complimentary.

"You were clever enough to blow up a moon and destroy two of our star destroyers. You should be able to do this." The middle Resh sat back and grinned, a movement that seemed to split his face in half. Two rows of razor-sharp teeth made it more of a grimace. The bulbous yellow eyes held glints of white and black.

"Won't they suspect something? After all, we were on a mountain and suddenly disappeared."

"You will be returned. The time for your furlough will be almost over, anyway. Your companions will have mind-altering drugs that will not only take away any memory of their time here but also have a conditioning to help you do the deed or kill you if you change your mind. Their lives depend on yours, Sub-Commander Diego Perez. And your life depends on theirs."

"What about the female Grrlock? She is not a member of the crew. How do I explain her?"

"She and the Turengen will stay here. Hostages, if you will. Our friends here will be on Grrlock to make sure you do your job well. If you don't, then the rest of the female Grrlock's family will be killed. If you say anything to your Grrlock friend, Ziron, or anyone else, we will kill the females.

At that, Diego glanced at the Grrlocks sitting nearby.

"Yes, they will be ready to do their job," the leader Resh said. "You may be from a backward planet, but I think you understand there are ways to know if you have said anything to anyone."

This matched what his dream had shown, except it had depicted him as being mind altered. Already, there was a difference. Why? Regardless, Rrishan and Fress were hostages. He would have to be careful. And no, he didn't doubt what they said. "You said, companions. If you are keeping two here, and Rreengrol is going back with me, why did you say companions? Who else is coming with us?"

"You and your shipmate will go back with Commander Hreeshan, just as you went on leave with him. He is the other member of your death squad. Do not doubt his willingness to make sure this job is done."

Commander Hreeshan? Despite the dream, it seemed unthinkable. Diego gazed at the three Resh. He didn't like what was happening, with or without his foretelling. He took a deep breath, then let it out in a discouraged sigh. "Very well. I will do it."

"Good. You really had little choice, mrees."

The Resh barked an order to the guard by the door. "Go with him." To Diego, he added, "Do not forget, you are a prisoner. Soon, we will return you to Grrlock. We will not be far away."

Without saying a word, Diego followed the guard out the door. Another guard outside fell in step behind him. When he entered the cell, Rreengrol was still unconscious. A quick exploration showed Diego that Rrishan and Fress weren't there. Then he smelled something funny. His head started pounding again, and within seconds, he slumped over and joined his friend.

CHAPTER FOURTEEN

Diego awoke in the tent next to Rreengrol. There was no Resh, no spaceship, and no squashed tent. Did he dream of the meeting this time, too? Diego tried to sit up and felt the pounding in his head, almost making him throw up. The headache told him his visit on the Resh ship was no dream. How could the Resh come this close to Grrlock without being detected?

Rain still pattered on the outside of the tent, but the inside was dry. There was a warmth in his palm, and he realized his hand was closed tightly enough to make his muscles hurt. He opened his fingers and found a jewel. It was tiny, bright red, and blinking. Diego peered closer and saw a word in the Seressin glyphs. 'Remember.' It blinked a few more times and then puffed into smoke. The warmth remained in his palm, but his headache slowly receded.

Without waking Rreengrol, Diego slipped out of the tent. He felt an icy breeze blowing his hair and rustling the branches above him. Even in the pre-dawn darkness, he could see the other tent was gone. Not just gone as though packed up recently, but as though it had never been there. How could he explain that one when they returned? He couldn't say anything to Lershan, but she would want to know what had happened to her cub.

"Commander Hreeshan has summoned us back to the ship," Rreengrol said behind him.

Diego jumped. "Don't sneak up on me like that!"

Rreengrol grinned. "We Grrlock can be silent when we choose."

Diego studied Rreengrol's face. He didn't look any different.

"Something wrong?" Rreengrol's tone was muted, but there was a subtle difference warning Diego.

"Your sister...."

"You were totally out, but all this frightened her, and she went back down the mountain. Fress went with her." Rreengrol snorted. "And to think she wanted to be a squire."

Diego ignored the last. "Your father is going to pick her up?"

Rreengrol shook his head. "Uncle Hrushan. They should be near his house by now. As I said, you were totally out."

"I remembered a weird dream."

"You woke me up, but you went right back to sleep."

"I guess I did. Sorry. I could have helped you."

With a shrug, Rreengrol said, "It wasn't that hard. Easier than putting them up, which reminds me. We need to break camp and head back down."

"Sure thing." Diego noticed the headache was almost gone by now. *Must be the fresh air.* There was a slight glow in the east.

"You didn't dream about Resh?"

"Why would I? Besides, Grrlocks almost never dream." Rreengrol frowned.

"Oh, I didn't know that."

"I guess that's the realm of humans and Seressin. Drop it."

"Um, all right." Diego would not swear by it, but Rreengrol seemed different. He couldn't chance doing anything wrong around him.

The wind died to a soft breeze, so taking down the tent was easy. It was still chilly in the pre-dawn, and Diego pulled on his all-weather jacket. Soon, they were taking a path leading to the downward trail. There were hints of dawn on the eastern horizon.

Diego said nothing. He had to assume everything the Resh said was true. He could count only on himself. Rreengrol led the way, not saying anything. It was mid-morning by the time they reached the trailhead.

To Diego's surprise, Hreeshan was waiting for them. "Rejas!"

"Hurry. We must get to the spaceport quickly."

Diego wanted to ask Rreengrol how he knew Hreeshan had summoned them but instead ventured a different question. "Is it permitted to ask why we are returning so quickly?"

Hreeshan nodded. "Supreme Commander Marzol is coming aboard the *Star Devourer* during the next cycle, and Commander Ziron wishes all his commanders and sub-commanders to be present. Where is the Turengen?"

"She went with Rreengrol's sister. Do we need to call her back in?" Diego asked, wondering what would happen if the commander said 'yes.'

"No. She is a first-year squire, so she can remain. I wonder at the wisdom of including females as squires."

Rreengrol snickered but said nothing.

Hreeshan had a vehicle at the parking area, and they loaded all their gear in the back. The Grrlock wasted no time on the road, driving it as fast as was feasible. By late afternoon, they reached the spaceport. Workers stowed their belongings, including the tents. Soon, they were on the shuttle, settled in, and ready to return to the ship.

Diego's gut clenched tighter and tighter as the shuttle began preparations for taking off. He had not the slightest idea what he was going to do when he arrived on the *Star Devourer*. He couldn't warn Marix Ziron, and he couldn't trust Commander Hreeshan and Rreengrol.

CHAPTER FIFTEEN

When the shuttle landed in the bay and powered down, Hreeshan turned to him. "The Supreme Commander is coming aboard just before last meal. It is now a little before second meal, ship's time. Report to Commander Ziron before you do anything else. Someone will take your belongings to your quarters. Squire Rreengrol comes with me, so we can discuss protocol. We will be in attendance for the Supreme Commander's conference with Commander Ziron after last meal."

Diego just bowed politely and proceeded to the command quarters. There was no one there, so he headed for the bridge, where he found Marix Ziron giving orders to various department heads. Diego stepped out of the way, waiting patiently.

When he finished, Ziron turned to his squire. "Ah, Quirlis. We cut your vacation a couple of cycles short."

That was probably as close to an apology he would get from the Seressin. Such was their way. "It is all right, Marix," Diego said, his mind churning.

"There will be other leaves, Diego. Right now, you have the next three hours free. Report back two hours after second meal, and we will go over the protocol for the visit of the Supreme Commander Marzor."

"Yes, sir."

Diego left but didn't know what to do for the next hour before lunch. Then he went to the study center. He should be able to do a tutorial without breaking the Resh's rules. In the center, he looked up anything available on mind control. Diego couldn't help but wonder just how the Resh would know if he had said anything to anyone other than Rreengrol or Hreeshan. The only way would be if they had done one of those implants on him. He didn't feel different, but Diego didn't know enough to tell. Would he automatically try to kill his marix? The information he found confused him and left him with more questions than answers.

Diego wasn't hungry, but he had missed breakfast, so he went down to the lower rank officers' mess hall. Nothing appealed to him, but he grabbed a couple of protein bars and then looked around to see if there was an empty table.

The only one was by the door. Diego sat and then stared at the protein bars. He felt someone by his side and looked up. Rreengrol.

His Grrlock friend grinned. "Someone else gets to cook the food today, but apparently, you aren't interested." He studied Diego, glancing at his breakfast.

Diego gazed at him, unable to figure out what Rreengrol was saying. Then he realized, "Guess I'm still tired. Too tired to eat, I suppose." He realized most of the time his Grrlock friend was still the same. Teasing was part of Rreengrol's normal behavior. He smiled. "You snored."

"Ha! You dreamed and woke me up!"

Bress joined them. "You came back early, but where is Fress?"

Knowing the Turengen's ability to read minds, Diego kept his answer simple. "With Rreengrol's sister."

"Commander Hreeshan said it was all right for Fress to continue her leave," Rreengrol added.

Bress cocked his head, then grinned. "I am sure she is enjoying her time on Grrlock."

Diego did his best to keep his mind clear, concentrating on

his lunch. He left before the others. Maybe he could do a little in the exercise room and then rest in his cabin for a bit. He wasn't getting closer to a solution by sitting in the messroom.

Up in the exercise room, he picked a saber, went through a few warmup exercises, and then practiced in front of a mirror. He imagined he was fighting the three Resh. Advancing, he dispatched one. Lunging dispatched another one. Diego slashed at the third one, which burst open like a piñata. If only it could be that easy.

He looked in the mirror and saw three Turengen behind him. Two he recognized—Bress and Jeng—and one he didn't recognize. "Bress? What are you all doing in here?"

"Something...." He tapped his otter-shaped head with one stubby finger. "Think."

Think? Diego just stared at the three creatures. Then he realized Bress had picked up enough in his mind to know not to discuss it out loud.

"By the way, this is my dam, Noress," Bress said.

"Glad to meet you, Noress."

"Commander. Bress says much good about you. Now you must think."

Diego was uncomfortable letting them read his mind in a common exercise area. What if Rreengrol came looking for him? The Grrlock might do something before he could figure out a solution to his dilemma. "Let's go to my cabin."

Bress tugged on his sleeve. "No, come with us. Cabin has been visited. Besides, we want to show you something. Something I do as a lowly commander!"

Why would someone visit his cabin unless they were looking for him? Certainly not Commander Ziron. Diego had the pin for that, he thought, reaching up and touching the device. A device.... A listening device, he wondered. All his things had been delivered to his cabin, so that was feasible.

Bress nodded. "Come. We have little time."

Diego put the saber away without cleaning it and followed the trio of otter people. They headed toward the shuttle bay. He remembered the last time he had been in the bay with the Turengen. They had believed him when everyone else thought he was a traitor during the Koress assignment. Diego had learned a great deal since then, but he was glad Commander Ziron had not given him command of a group or operation yet. As this incident with the Resh proved, there was still so much to learn.

Bress showed him into the command deck of the craft, pointing to the control center. "Working to make this easier to pilot. If there is an emergency, even a squire can work the controls." The Turengen pointed to the pilot's chair. Diego sat down.

"Think," Noress commanded him.

Think! he heard in his mind. Soft but distinct. Diego almost jumped out of his chair in surprise. Noress climbed into his lap.

"You helped our family become successful... Think."

Diego thought, going over everything from his dream to his confrontation with the Resh on their ship, to his return to *Star Devourer*. Jeng had a small portable computer and was deftly tapping into it. Diego's final thought was worrying the Resh could know what was in his mind—his interaction with the Turengen.

They...not in your mind. Nothing to interfere with your thoughts.

Diego breathed a sigh of relief.

But...not know about listening devices.

Which was why they were in his mind. Noress was still on his lap, her dark eyes boring into his. Bress had climbed into the co-pilot's seat. He chittered to his dam, then jumped over to join her on his lap. The weight was uncomfortable but not painful.

Let Commander Ziron know we would like to meet the Supreme Commander. We helped save High Commanders.

Yes, he thought. *And I will have weapons I need to protect*

Lord Ziron. And the supreme leader.

Do not count on that.

Diego was surprised. If he couldn't take any weapons, then how would Rreengrol and Hreeshan be able to take weapons?

Do not know. Will do our best. Remember to invite. Dam will try to stay close enough to 'hear' you.

Yes. What if Marix Ziron will not allow you?

Will figure something out. We believe you as we believed you before.

Now Diego felt a bit of hope. Not much of a plan, but better than he had before he met with Bress and the others. He glanced at his watch. Time to meet Commander Ziron. The Turengen slipped off his lap, and he headed up toward the marix's cabin.

Diego had just exited the elevator when he almost literally ran into Rreengrol.

"What were you doing in the shuttle area?"

CHAPTER SIXTEEN

"I had free time," Diego snapped, irritated at the intrusion of the Resh through his friend. "So, I did as I pleased. Besides, Commander Lurin had said something about improvements, and I wanted to see what he was talking about."

"What improvements?"

"In piloting. The instruments are easier to reach, read, and use. Why the interrogation? It was bad enough to have to take a junior squire to your planet without having a senior one keep checking up on me."

Rreengrol paused for a moment, and then his green eyes narrowed. "We know, and so do you," he said in a low voice. "It will be done." He paused again, and when his eyes widened, he almost appeared normal. "Don't want you to get into trouble with the marix."

"I won't if I get there soon. See you later," Diego said, more nonchalantly than he felt. He continued down the corridor at a jog. At the door of the multi-purpose hall, Diego placed his hand on the ident plate. The door opened, and he slipped in.

"I thought you had forgotten your obligation," Ziron said tersely.

Obviously, his commander was nervous. Diego would have to be careful with Marix Ziron as well. "The fault is mine. I am here to do what you need."

The reception hall was the only thing on the ship that

could be considered opulent, being two stories high. It had enough space to accommodate a herd of cattle. Even the generic decorations looked costly. Ziron could order the brightly hued windows to change to monitors showing the outside stars. The floors were a combination of polished wood and burnished metal. Unlike the rest of the ship, lights hung from the ceiling, something like the chandeliers of his father's hacienda. While it might be below what the supreme commander of the Seressin Empire was used to, this ought to be impressive and fitting for a reception.

"I believe from what you have told me, you were at least a little used to entertaining on a grand scale insofar as you could on a primitive planet."

"Yes, Marix. My father was a man of position, and he often entertained."

"While I go over the agendas and the papers Serix Marzor wants to discuss after the reception, you will prepare this room for the reception."

"Yes, sir. How long will the reception last? And will there be a dinner in here first?"

"No dinner, but a table of the serix's favorite foods would be in order. Appetizers and his favorite drinks. And not flame juice." Ziron smiled at the reference to an early incident when Diego was serving the commander. "The cooks will know."

"It will be done." Diego remembered Bress's request. "Sir, who is allowed to attend this reception?"

"Only the most senior squires. All sub-commanders and commanders. It will be brief. The serix will speak, and then Commander Hreeshan and I will remain while everyone else is dismissed."

Which meant that if he didn't do the job the Resh required, then Hreeshan would.

However, Bress could attend, as well as Jeng and a few other Turengen. "Thank you, Marix. I will get busy right now."

"Have some of the trusted squires help set this up," Ziron said as he exited the room.

The first thing Diego did was to find out about Serix Marzor's tastes in food and drink. The act of placing food and drink on a table seemed straightforward. But there had to be something to distract attention from whatever he or Bress needed to do. What better thing than a bit of celebration from a backward planet? Paper lanterns, or the equivalent, perhaps something akin to a small band. He had not paid attention to what kind of music Seressins liked. Of course, dancing was out of the question.

"My understanding is that only the serix, marix, and Commander Hreeshan will be in attendance after the crowd leaves," the cook, a Seressin who appeared to be about the same age as Lurin, rumbled.

"Yes, so there is no need for many refreshments."

"Good. Just plenty of Seressin bil-wallor wine."

Diego grinned. "Yes." Then he called Commander Lurin and asked for some of his squires to report to the conference hall. He also asked the commander what was available for decorating tastefully.

Lurin's roar of laughter boomed through the communicator. "Seressins do nothing fancy!"

Diego could dispute that, considering all the medals and other decorations Marix Ziron wore when he went planet-side on Koress.

"I will have my Turengen squires bring what they can find," he assured Diego.

"Thank you, Commander Lurin." As he returned to the hall, Diego saw Commander Hreeshan and Rreengrol.

Diego greeted the commander.

"How are you planning on making this a fitting place for the serix of the Seressin Empire?" Hreeshan asked.

"If the means are available, I wish to have a few decorations resembling what my people use for celebrations." At Hreeshan's doubtful gaze, Diego added. "Nothing silly. I would never have a piñata or anything like that, but something colorful. Something to show that we are entertaining a person of importance."

"As long as it doesn't interfere," Hreeshan said. He turned to Rreengrol. "Stay and help Quirlis Diego."

"Of course, Commander." When Hreeshan left, presumably toward Marix Ziron's quarters, Rreengrol asked, "So what would you like me to do?"

"Get the refreshment table ready," Diego said. There was nothing else they could do now. He found an elegant covering for the table, and they brought out the wines and bowls of food. A group of Turengens and other creatures came through the door, carrying piles of wall hangings in their arms.

Diego dug through the decorations and showed where they could be attached to the walls. The garlands were not as colorful as he would have liked, but they were festive enough for someone whose taste he wasn't sure of.

Think, a tiny voice said in his mind.

So, Diego passed along what he had learned from Commander Ziron. There was a smallish hint of pleasure but no answer. He watched the decorations going up and made suggestions. Rreengrol eagerly helped. Diego had a momentary thought that he was missing something. Something important.

An hour and a half before the Supreme Commander's shuttle was supposed to dock, Marix Ziron came back and examined the progress in the hall. He gazed at the decorations and huffed. Knowing how austere the commander's own quarters were, Diego figured the marix was not overly impressed with the extras.

"This should please Serix Marzor," he said, to Diego's surprise. "Now all sub-commanders and commanders change into dress uniforms and return quickly. No weapons except ceremonial sabers. You will not be here that long, just long enough for the serix to greet you."

Diego hastened to his quarters, cleaned up, and donned his sub-commander's uniform. He clipped his saber onto his belt and wondered just how he would accomplish or stop an assassination with a sword. When he stepped out of his cabin, he met Rreengrol.

"You look fit to meet a Seressin supreme commander," he said jovially. "Here. It won't register on the weapons check monitors."

In an equally low voice, Diego asked, "You have one, too?"

"Of course." And he sauntered away toward the hall.

Diego felt the thing in his hand. It was the size of his palm and the shape of a flattened egg. He glanced down and saw a bilious green color of all but a tiny point that stuck out from the smaller end. A metallic nubbin was right in the middle of the weapon, and Diego figured it made the weapon fire. He pocketed it and then followed his friend.

Rreengrol met Hreeshan, and they walked between the guards at the door to the great hall. Each of the guards held a box-like device in their hands, presumably making sure no one had any unauthorized weapons. Lurin stood just inside the door.

If he could have brought something to defend Commander Ziron and Supreme Commander Marzor, he'd have tossed the tiny weapon away. He didn't. Shaking his head, Diego continued toward the door and the two huge Seressin guards. He knew them, had seen them before. In fact, one was the guard he had talked to on his first night as Marix Ziron's squire. That didn't make him feel less anxious.

He walked between them, and the boxes turned red and let out a noise that wasn't loud but unmistakably audible. The guards leaped forward and grabbed him by the arms. One of them squeezed his wrist and jerked away the tiny weapon. "This is Resh manufacture and, as such, treason!"

Lurin pivoted and held him by the throat. "I will take care of this soft-skinned turncoat myself. Good work, men!"

CHAPTER SEVENTEEN

Diego tried to say something to Lurin—to explain. However, Lurin had one enormous fist wrapped around Diego's throat, squeezing tight enough to send him into unconsciousness. The tips of the sharp claws dug into his skin. He wheezed in enough air to stay awake. He *had* to stay awake. Lurin's other fist had grabbed his sub-commander's uniform, pulling it tight enough to constrict his ribcage. He tried to pry the fingers away, but a roar from the Seressin made him stop. Diego chose instead to go limp.

It became obvious he was not supposed to be the assassin, but why had the Resh recruited him? Why had they threatened him and made promises they would not keep? Of course, he knew they would not keep their promises, anyway. But his arrest also wasn't in his dream. In the dream, he killed the supreme commander. Rreengrol and Hreeshan helped him and had been killed trying to escape. So, what happened? What was his purpose now? Was he supposed to provide a diversion so Hreeshan and Rreengrol could do the job under Resh control? Or were they really under control? He had to tell Lurin. This was more than a plot to discredit him—he knew it.

"I will take him to the detention," another Seressin marching beside them said. It was a sub-commander Diego didn't recognize.

"No, I will take care of this scum myself. And no one will mind in the least if there is nothing on the floor but a smear,"

Lurin roared. He dragged Diego into an elevator, only letting go of his uniform enough to push the controls of the elevator.

When the door opened, Diego thought he recognized the squire's quarters—his first duty station. Lurin dragged him to an empty squire's cabin and dropped him on the floor. Diego tried to suck in air through his bruised windpipe, coughing and hacking painfully.

"We have little time."

"I know," Diego choked out. Then he jerked up. "Time for what?"

Lurin growled. "To save the commanders, you idiot."

"You know?"

"Quick. Take this," a chittering voice said.

In confusion, Diego looked up and saw Bress holding out his stubby hand. There was a small weapon, but this one he recognized and felt confident taking. Bress handed him another weapon, and Diego took this one, too. It was a gas bomb that incapacitated but didn't kill. Usually. Diego gazed at Lurin.

"This is all I can do. The rest is up to you and the Turengen. You have little time. The Supreme Commander's shuttle has called, and it is approaching. It will come alongside soon, and I must get back to the reception hall."

"How...."

"How do you think, you mammalian softling?" Lurin nodded toward the Turengen and then backed out of the room and headed to the elevator.

"Thanks, Bress. The dream I've had is filled full of laser blasts by now. Nothing seems to match what I saw when I was asleep," Diego said, still rubbing his throat. "But apparently, Rreengrol and Hreeshan have the directives to assassinate Marix Ziron and Serix Marzor. How are we going to get back in there? You have access to the hall as a sub-commander."

"Not going in as a sub-commander. It will be hard for you, but we must go through the electrician's access," Bress said. He tapped his head. "Heard much. Will explain on the way. Hurry, hurry!"

Diego noticed Jeng and another Turengen. He got to his feet and sucked in a deep breath. "Let's go."

Bress, Jeng, and Mreff, another one of Bress's cousins, led the way to a difficult-to-see doorway recessed into the wall near the elevator. Even the Turengens had to bend a little to go through the small access. Diego got on his hands and knees. His throat ached, but he was sure other things would ache by the time he had finished crawling through this thing. He noticed the rungs of a ladder attached to the side of the well.

"Will tell you in your mind. *Jeng will go ahead, and Mreff and I will follow."*

The rungs were far enough apart the Turengen had to leap up. They were close enough to be awkward for Diego, but the foursome got into a cadence, so they made steady progress. He figured if this was an alternate route, then going up the elevator, they had some serious climbing to do.

Partially correct. This is also for fixing elevators and other electrical things nearby.

"Oh. How far...."

Try to think questions, but mostly listen. We will be tired when we get there.

Diego saw a picture of a kind of map of where they were going. He almost groaned.

Mreff is squire. Same group as Fress. He was around Commander Hreeshan sometimes and sometimes Sub-Commander Rreengrol. Your dream changed before you returned to the ship.

Diego tried to remember what had happened before. In the dream, he refused to do anything for the Resh. He also remembered they had used some kind of drug. Perhaps that was where it changed, when he agreed to help them.

Would make sense. But if they could mind alter you, they would. Can only think they cannot. And Hreeshan and Rreengrol are not only supposed to kill Commander Ziron and Supreme Commander Marzor but to destroy the ship.

"What?"

"Shh!"

Are they under control, or are they doing this on their own? Are they cooperating with the Resh? Diego couldn't believe it was the latter, but he had to know.

Hard to tell when thoughts are their own thoughts and when they are from control, but think the Resh are making them.

So that's why we have the gas grenades. To put them to sleep before they can do anything with the bombs, Diego thought.

Yes. But Lurin is going to be ready to take the device Hreeshan has and neutralize it.

Something bothered Diego. If the two Grrlocks were under control, they would destroy the entire ship, including themselves. Wouldn't they be able to detonate the devices if something wasn't going right? How could their little group overcome that problem? How were the Grrlocks being controlled? The Resh leader said something about implants. If the Resh could use the implants, couldn't the Seressin? Would Anaar, the android teacher, have an idea how to control the devices?

Diego felt a tug on his pants. He looked down into the dimness of the access tunnel and could barely make out Bress's whiskery face.

Mreff is going to talk to Anaar. Not much time. He will hurry, but perhaps you will be the best one to distract while Jeng and I use the gas.

Diego continued climbing. That his two friends could destroy the entire ship was mindboggling. Hreeshan had a mate and Rreengrol, a sister whose lives depended on making the Resh happy. Then Diego realized that the only way to make the Resh happy was to destroy the Seressin Empire. Perhaps this was what was happening here. What better way to demoralize the Seressin hierarchy?

Yes, that is probably so. Demoralize and put into chaos.

The tiny access seemed too narrow, but he figured it could be his imagination. Diego's shoulders and hands ached, but he couldn't stop. He felt a headache beginning again but pushed the throbbing back as much as he could. There was no room for error here. Despite any discomfort, he didn't slow down.

"Ssst, leave ladder soon and go through horizontal access," Jeng whispered.

She must have realized Diego still had trouble figuring out who was thinking. *Okay,* he thought back, watching to see where she went. He could barely see her feet, but when he blinked, they were gone, and Diego felt for the other passageway. Dim light flickered ahead of him, and he knew that was where Jeng went.

Yes, yes!

Now, he was on his hands and knees, and the twinges grew into something more unwelcome. No matter. They had to get there in time. Diego just hoped he could move once he left these passageways.

Not much further.

Diego said nothing. There was nothing to say. He was a little dismayed he was making noise, but there was a murmuring of sound ahead growing louder as they approached, and the light grew brighter as well.

We come to another ladder. We go down. Will take us to the kitchen area. I will go out first. One gas grenade will neutralize the cooks and staff. You will come out when I say to.

All right, Diego agreed. He started up the ladder, feeling his heart hammer halfway up his throat. He wondered about their plan or lack of it. If they stopped Commander Hreeshan and Rreengrol, how would they rescue Rreengrol's family, Fress, and Hreeshan's family? How could they fool the Resh? Diego sighed. One thing at a time.

As they climbed, he could hear the cooks and servers in the kitchen area. Diego remembered his experience with the flame juice when he first became Marix Ziron's squire. He didn't remember one of these access places.

Storage area. I am at the bottom. Be careful and wait.

Again, Diego didn't answer. He didn't hear Jeng leaving but heard a soft choking, several thuds, and then silence. Following the instructions, Diego waited. It wasn't long, although it seemed an eternity. He felt his muscles tighten up and then used the calming exercises taught by — Commander Hreeshan. There had to be a way to save the Grrlocks. There had to be.

CHAPTER EIGHTEEN

Come.

Speed was the only consideration. Diego dropped the last few feet and then got down on his hands and knees. Crawling out, he saw various beings he recognized as cooks, a few Seressin, and a Breanth guard lying on the floor. The Breanth gave him an idea.

"A disguise," he muttered.

"Worth trying, friend Diego," Bress commented.

With no further comment, Diego stripped the guard of his outer accouterments. The armor went on over his uniform and then the headpiece, which also had a communicator. Diego listened to the chatter but refused to respond. The Serix Marzor's shuttle had docked, and the supreme commander was on his way to the audience hall. Diego gathered the guard's weapons and marched to the door. The uniform was heavy and somewhat large, but putting it on over his uniform helped it fit. The helmet would serve as a deterrent to the gas. Diego handed his own portable mask to the Turengen. He needed his hands free.

Bress looked up at him. "Not bad. Not good, but not bad." The Turengen chittered his laughter.

"Don't laugh. "I'll be blasted if they recognize me too quickly," he exclaimed. Diego didn't have the features of a Breanth, but he dipped the front of the helmet to hide some of his humanness. Hopefully, with the crowd gathered in the hall, going unnoticed would be easier. The helmet communicator erupted with demands for all the guards.

"Here," Jeng said, handing him a bottle.

"What's this?"

"A seasoning, but the powder sticks and is brown. Will help disguise you a little."

Pouring a bit in his hand, Diego sniffed it. It wasn't pepper to make him sneeze. He rubbed some on his cheeks and the rest of his face. It stung, but he ignored it.

"Better," Bress declared. "You go out now, and we will follow."

Diego clumped toward the door as the communicator announced the supreme commander was only a few minutes away from the hall. Commander Ziron waited near the entrance. Diego needed to hurry. He took a deep breath and strode through the sliding door with more confidence than he felt.

Moving past the guards and the sub-commanders waiting in the back, Diego tried to see the supreme commander. He slid along the wall until he was only a few paces from Ziron, then he stopped. Rreengrol was not in sight, but he saw Hreeshan standing to the marix's left. Hreeshan glanced around, but his gaze didn't rest on Diego. It rested on someone to his left.

Leaning against the wall, Diego did his own study of the crowd. He saw Rreengrol nearby, moving closer to the entrance. It was stifling with all the waiting beings. Lowering his voice, he growled, "It's too crowded at the door. All non-essential personnel move back!"

Good!

Bress?

Yes, be ready! Do not forget. The helmet will protect you if you lower the shield.

Diego edged closer to Rreengrol until he was almost beside him. His friend was in his Sub-Commander uniform, but he appeared to have a larger stomach. The device? Rreengrol's gaze fixated on the door, and he didn't pay attention to Diego.

Then another guard, as well as the communicator, blasted out, "Stand at attention for the Supreme Commander."

Armor and ceremonial equipment clinked as everyone came to attention. Diego could feel Rreengrol stiffen next to him, pulling in a deep breath. Was it all Resh, or was there anything of his Grrlock friend trying to fight for control?

"Remember Rrishan, Shennel, and Lershan," he whispered. Rreengrol stiffened and then moaned. The door slid open, and Diego saw, out of the corner of his eye, Rreengrol reaching down to his stomach.

He couldn't wait and lowered the helmet shield. "Remember Rrishan," he repeated. Then he grabbed his friend's wrists, pulling him back against the wall. Rreengrol had the same training he had, so he fought back, but not as effectively as Diego figured he would. Diego used his helmet to head-butt Rreengrol, and when his friend slid to the ground, unconscious, he leaped for Hreeshan.

"Remember your mate, Hreeshan," he shouted, hitting him at knee level, the armor adding force. With a howl of pain, the commander went down.

Noxious green gas permeated the room. Bress leaped over Hreeshan and slid out the closing door.

Only then did Diego realize the supreme commander remained outside the door. Ziron roared his anger and defiance. A bolt of energy blasted past his shoulder, close enough for him to feel the heat. Diego rolled along the floor and leaped over several unconscious commanders.

Shouting into the communicator, Diego faced his commander. "Marix! A plot. The Resh infiltrated and were going to destroy you and the supreme commander!"

"You are the traitor!"

"No! The Resh captured and tried to recruit me, but I never intended to do their bidding."

Ziron leaped for him, and Diego let his commander power him to the ground. The armor protected his head, but he still felt as though a bull had trampled him. "I had a dream. Like before...." Not the entire truth, but close enough.

As though slapped, Ziron drew back. The fist aimed for Diego's nose stopped in mid-air. "What?" The room had grown silent except for Jeng's pattering feet and the clumping of several guards.

Great, thought Diego. *Some of them had thought of everything, including gas masks.*

"You need to leave the ship, Marix Ziron. You and the supreme commander, Diego, and the Turengen," a voice behind him rumbled. Lurin! "This really is a Resh plot. The Grrlocks were mind-tampered by the Resh to blow up the ship and everyone in it. Somehow, the human escaped the tampering."

Ziron got up, gazing at Diego but talking to Lurin. "He isn't compromised?"

"No, Commander," Jeng replied. "Could feel nothing out of the ordinary. Saw his mind on Koress. No difference."

"Marix, trust me," Lurin implored. "And trust him. I must defuse these bombs. You need to be away."

Ziron growled, "All right. Let's go." Using his special access code, the Seressin opened the door, and the three of them walked right into a contingent of the serix's guards.

CHAPTER NINETEEN

The first guard reached for Diego. "This one…"

"This one is my squire. Sub-commander Diego Perez," Ziron bellowed. "This assassination plot is not over, but my squire and his companions have bought the supreme commander time to escape."

The home world guard stared at Diego for a few seconds.

"Move to the shuttle to protect your commander, or move aside so we can."

"Come, but if there is any move to do anything to the supreme commander, we will kill both of you. Those are the ultimate orders of the Serix Home Guard." As though seeing the awkwardness of what he had just said to a commanding officer, the Seressin guard continued, "Serix Marzor sent us back to help you, Commander Ziron, but not the human," he said, pointing to Diego.

"Come," Ziron ordered, ignoring the guard's last comment. The company ran down the corridor, squeezed into an elevator, and then ran to the main shuttle bay.

Diego had been thinking as they rushed toward the supreme commander's shuttle. What would happen when the Resh realized their plot had failed? He knew Commander Lurin could disarm the devices, but how quickly would the Resh know? Would they then kill Rreengrol's family, Hreeshan's, and Fress?

The hatch to the Supreme Commander's craft stood open.

Diego could feel the rumble of the engines ready to engage.

"Marix," he panted as they reached the ramp. "I must take another ship. Something needs to explode for the Resh to think their plot worked!"

Ziron stepped into the hatch behind the guards. "What?"

Bress stood behind Ziron.

"We need to go now!!" a guard shouted from the Serix Marzor's ship.

"Marix. What Diego says is true. I will go with Squire Diego," the Turengen chittered. "Many hostages. All murdered if you and serix are not killed in the planned destruction of the ship."

Ziron growled in apparent frustration. "Obviously, the only way I am going to know what's going on is to come with you." He made a quick motion with his claws to those inside the shuttle. "Get out of here. Now! Get the serix to safety."

Diego and Bress didn't wait for the rest of Ziron's orders. They dashed to the marix's personal shuttle. It took only a second to get inside since he had the code. "Bress, can you start up the engines?"

"Yes. What are your plans?"

"What plans?"

Bress coughed. "Exactly. No moons nearby to destroy."

Diego booted up the computers and typed in some commands. "Maybe there's something better."

Bress squeaked. "This?"

"Reading my thoughts again?"

"Can't help it. And what will we be doing in the meantime?"

"Isn't there an escape pod?"

"Sure, there is."

Commander Ziron stomped through the hatch, several more Turengen skittering in between his legs, including Jeng. The reptile man latched it behind him. "All right. What is going on?" he snapped.

Diego started telling him the entire story, even as he prepped the ship for take-off.

"Give the control room this code," Ziron interrupted, snapping off a string of numbers and glyphs.

Diego punched in the code. He and Bress maneuvered the shuttle for a quick departure, not too much after the serix's ship. He finished telling his marix what had happened and then presented his ideas.

"So, you propose to destroy this ship to fool the Resh? That is not only foolish but wasteful."

"Marix, begging your pardon, but what would be wasteful would be to let these Resh kill Seressin citizens and come back later to finish the job they had wanted me, Rreengrol, and Commander Hreeshan to do. I don't think they'd mess it up the next time. And I don't want Fress and Rrishan, Rejas Hreeshan's mate, or Rreengrol's family to die thinking they were abandoned." Diego paused for a second, then spoke in a fervent tone. "I don't want the Resh to feel like they can take us, and manipulate us, and then slide into some dark corner to gloat."

"Hmm. So, if the Resh think their plot has succeeded, they won't expect us to come for our people. Maybe they won't kill them right away."

"Yes, sir. We'll have a little time to plan a raid."

Ziron sat down in the command chair and rubbed his cheek patches. "Take us out, Sub-commanders Bress and Diego. The rest of the crew man the weaponry and life support systems."

"Yes, sir!" The four otter people scattered to their duty stations.

After the ship was far enough away, Ziron turned to Diego. "You realize, Quirlis, that this vessel will make a big enough bang to alert the Grrlock monitoring station but not enough to make them think there has been large destruction. It certainly won't fool the Resh."

"Yes, sir, but their agents are on Grrlock. If they think...."

Ziron scratched the corner of his chair with his main claw. "But how will we make them think my starship has blown up? There is only the fifth planet we are orbiting, and we certainly will not blow that up. Don't have the firepower, anyway."

"All the shuttles?" Diego ventured.

"No," Ziron growled.

Diego thought, but his mind seemed sluggish. Then, an alarming thought penetrated. "Would they be able to tell the serix's ship has left your ship, Marix?"

"If they have precise instruments, they should." His yellow eyes blinked. "Contact the supreme commander's ship and have them line up behind my ship so the *Star Devourer* is between them and Grrlock. It's not much, but until we can think of something else. Both ships need to stay in a stationary orbit on the far side of the planet, Grreng."

"I am picking up a vessel approaching slowly," Jeng called out. "From the outer rim of the Grrlock solar system."

"Give me the specifications," Ziron ordered.

"A private class ship. Unknown origin." Jeng paused and peered closer to the monitor. He punched in more commands. "One of the biggest privately owned ships I have ever seen, sir," Jeng chittered. "Mass approximately five million derchins."

At the helm, Diego jerked up in surprise. That was enormous for a private ship. He did the quick math — four million kilograms. That made it almost half the size of Commander Ziron's ship.

"Getting more readings," Jeng said. "It is well protected with advanced armament."

"Is it signaling?"

"No, sir," Jeng responded. "It's quiet."

Ziron grabbed the headset from the arm of his chair and listened. "No, it's nothing I've ever heard before. I'm sending a coded message to the serix." He listened a while longer and then typed in some code into his command chair keyboard.

No one said anything for several minutes. "Getting a coded message from the serix's shuttle, Marix Ziron. For you, sir," the Turengen on the communications console announced.

Ziron didn't answer; he worked the keyboard with both hands and listened on the headset. Finally, he punched up a command and jerked off the headphones.

A Seressin's voice thundered over the ship's communicator. "...not a request. This is a command. Report to *Star Devourer*!

With a sigh, Ziron stood up. "You are in command, Diego. Keep a close eye on that ship. Move out to within two million srechins. Make sure it doesn't get too close."

"Yes, sir." His gut clenched, knotting into something that seemed intent on making him throw up what little he had eaten today. But he couldn't. As before, he had to keep up the pretense of a fearless sub-commander.

"If it does, you will do everything you can to keep it from the serix." Marix Ziron clumped toward the exit and left the control room. Soon, they heard the soft whoosh of the escape pod hatch.

Diego turned his attention to the approaching ship. Over and above his churning stomach and growing headache, it gave him a bad feeling.

CHAPTER TWENTY

"Can you detect any weapons?" Diego asked.

Jeng chittered to herself for a few seconds. "All ships have basic weaponry," she finally answered. "But checking more." Then she muttered. "Shields. Yes...."

"What is it?" Diego asked.

"There are anomalies in the engine signature and some of the weaponry. They are like basic weapons, and yet they are different," Bress elaborated.

"Take us out. As though we were leaving the system. Different trajectory, but towards the ship. Keep checking the sensors."

"Yes, sir," the Turengen, who had taken over Diego's place on the helm controls, answered.

"Shrish, right?" Diego asked.

"Yes, sir!" She wiggled her whiskers to show her pleasure.

Diego nodded and kept gazing at the monitors.

"The engine seems to use something different from ours," Jeng reported. "A different configuration. Maybe a different kind of engine."

"What kind?"

She shook her head. "Unknown. They are changing their course slightly to stay within two million srechins."

That suited him. They could still monitor the other ship while staying safe. Still, something about the other ship kept him on edge. "Maintain the same course, ahead three-quarter light speed." If they got all the way to a wormhole portal, then they would have called his bluff. They continued on a course that had them parallel to the other ship but out of range of their weapons. No one said anything for some time.

"Ship has increased speed as well," Jeng reported.

The ship continued out of the system as though ignoring them. "Increase to match. Monitor their systems."

Bress screeched just as a monitor lit up in an eye-blinding flash. He rubbed his eyes and shook his head.

Diego swiped a hand over his eyes. "By the saints, what was that?"

"Ship exploded!" Jeng cried.

It wasn't the ship they were following. The explosion was aft. Diego's stomach knotted even more. "*Star Devourer*?"

Bress moaned. "Yes. Yes."

"The serix's ship?"

"Can't tell. Too bright. They were too close. Had to be hit. Had to...."

Diego pulled up the communications console and called the *Star Devourer*, then the serix's ship. He heard nothing but static. Marix Ziron, Lurin, all his friends, Rreengrol, Hreeshan. All gone.

Jeng cut into his misery. "The ship we are following slowed, but it is now increasing speed to leave the system."

With a growl, Diego turned his attention back to the monitor. "Did you find out anything else about it?"

Jeng shook her head and then stopped, stared a moment, and began chittering.

"What?"

"It uses the.... No, it can't be."

"What?" Diego repeated. By now, everyone was staring at the young Turengen.

"Spiral energy."

Diego took a couple of seconds to understand what Jeng said. He couldn't. "What is spiral energy?"

"The computer explains better than I can."

Diego read what Jeng sent to his screen. Scientists discovered twin black holes near the edge of the galaxy they believe were slowly merging. Right now, they were spiraling around each other in a tight orbit, throwing off incredible amounts of energy.

"I do not understand how it works," Jeng commented. "Scientists say the energy could provide much power, but they don't know how to control it in a ship. Some scientists claim there is an element in the galaxy that contains it."

Bress snorted. "Someone has figured it out."

Diego took a couple more seconds to think of alternatives. They were alone, trailing a ship using an unknown type of power. "I would really like to know where this ship is going, but obviously, we can't catch up to them. Does anyone have any suggestions that might cause them to slow down?"

"Could we pretend the explosion did something to us? Fool the other ship?" Bress suggested.

"Been done, but I don't have any other ideas." Diego sighed. "Explode an implosion torpedo aft. Full forward in a spin. We won't lose anything trying. If anyone has a better idea that might make them think we are poor, pathetic survivors of a massive explosion, let me know. Make sure you have your harnesses tight."

As the last syllable popped out of his mouth, the ship shook, and then the monitor showed they were in a headlong spin, heading toward the other ship. No one said anything for several minutes.

Then Jeng announced, "They have slowed to three-quarter light."

"Cut our engines and drift. We'll see what they do."

"Yes, sir," Bress answered.

As he had before, Diego felt inadequate sitting in Commander Ziron's chair. Of course, Commander Ziron wasn't around anymore. Despite the rough way Seressins treated each other and especially treated their subordinates and slaves, he would miss his marix. He felt cut off. The *Star Devourer* had become his new home. Now, it was gone. Anger smoldered in his chest, then flame. He determined the Resh would find out who they were dealing with.

He realized his attention had wandered, and he blinked, gazing at his Turengen crew. They were staring at him. "I have nothing left with the commander gone. I only want to find the Resh planet and figure out a way to save Rrishan and Fress or...."

"We are your crew. We have nothing, either. We will follow," Bress said. All the otter people said the last sentence together.

Diego turned back to the monitors and saw the large ship continuing out of the system. "Keep it on the monitors as long as you can. Is there any way to tell their destination through the wormhole?"

"Our computers can guess."

Diego nodded. "As soon as they pass through a gate, go to top speed. And have the computers work on their guesses."

"Yes, sir. And where are we going, Commander?" Jeng asked.

"Resh." Diego looked at his monitor. His last time in command, he had several more qualified crew members, a full complement. Now? Five Turengen and a green commander.

"They have gone through the gate."

"Lay in coordinates for the Resh system," he ordered. "And when we pass through the gate, see if you can pick up something—telepathically."

"Yes, sir," Bress said. "Commander, what if they are waiting on the other side? The computer is sure they are going to Resh."

"Good point. I should have thought of that. You are right. Is there a nearby gate to another destination? And then to Resh?"

"Yes, Commander."

"Let's do it." He hoped no one was guarding the other gate. "Arm all weapons as well. We'll be ready for anyone."

"Prill, man the weapons!" Bress chittered.

Diego continued to watch the monitors. He tapped into his personal computer — or Commander Ziron's, rather. No, his, he reminded himself. He had worked with Anaar in the months since the defeat of the Resh in the Koress system to learn the various technological systems used in the control rooms of most Seressin ships. His mind still whirled with all the information coming over his computer screen and the monitors. He wished he had time to assimilate all the information.

"Ask," Bress chittered softly. "Just ask."

Sometimes, the Turengen's ability helped; at other times, it intruded. Diego knew their survival now depended on the otter-people's abilities. He swallowed his pride. "What is the probability someone might wait on the other side of the gate?"

"If we go in the same passageway, which is closest to Resh, close to one hundred percent, sir," Prill answered. "If we go into the Franjin System, maybe thirty percent."

Diego sighed. "We have to take the chance on the Franjin passageway. Do it. Be ready for an ambush."

"Yes, sir."

Several hours later, they slipped through a small wormhole to a comparatively small system. Franjin was a dwarf sun with several insignificant planets swinging close to it. Several dead rocky planets tumbled in the system's far reaches.

A distant outpost on the first planet barely registered in range of their sensors. If the station could detect them, Diego would not worry about it. "Where is the nearest gate that will take us to Resh?"

"Two million srechins. The next gate will take us into the

Resh system near the influence of the Resh sun. Almost the same orbit as the innermost planet. We will be uncomfortable for a while, but we will survive, and it will be harder for the Resh to detect us as we enter."

Not far as stellar distances went, Diego thought. And it was something that would improve the odds. "Good. Let's go." As they traveled, he checked the status of the weapons system. Several torpedoes, fore-and-aft laser cannons, and various concussive devices. The shields were fully operative as well. It was a well-stocked ship, fitting for Commander Ziron's fighter craft.

Diego watched the Turengen at their stations, amazed at their adaptability. Then his mind side-slipped to the incident on Koress when he had been accused of cowardice — of deserting his comrades. And there had been a vid to show his desertion. Anaar had explained how they had created the false vid. All through computer magic — making the false appear real. Was it possible here? Could their ship appear like something else, a different ship to any who were watching? Would it be possible for their computers to make their ship look like something else?

"Krim?" Diego turned to the Turengen most adept with computers.

"Yes, Commander."

"How much would sensors see about our ship right now?"

"They would see this is a Seressin ship of great capability, superior defenses, weaponry, and engine capacity." Her dark eyes were questioning.

"Did you get the computer read-outs for that other ship?"

"Yes, sir."

"Is there any way for the computers to make our ship look or seem different from what it is?"

"Like an electronic disguise?" Krim asked.

"Yes."

"I can try. It is complicated."

"If you can just confuse anyone watching, it would be helpful."

"I will do my best. It helps we have a little time before the next passageway."

It remained silent for several minutes. Diego realized going into the Resh System without a plan amounted to suicide. Krim said they would come in near the Resh sun.

"Commander?" Bress stood in front of Diego's command chair.

"Yes?"

"What do we do when we get to the Resh System?"

Diego gazed a moment at the Turengen. "I was trying to figure that out. Let me think a bit more. If there is no way to go in without a way to succeed, then we'll not go in," he said bluntly.

Bress nodded.

Diego realized he had no knowledge about the Resh planet or the place where he had been taken. Now, he needed to do some research.

Diego investigated the computer search module and typed in Resh, then home system. The star was a bright, large red disc. Six planets. No asteroids, although there were a few closely bunched dwarf planets revolving around each other.

The second world was the Resh home world. Nine-tenths oceans, lakes, and other bodies of water. No ice caps. The oceans varied in color from deep blue to deep green. The Resh capital lay underwater near a large island containing a spaceport and administrative buildings. Were they taken there? If that was the case, how could they get in and get their friends out undetected? With a sigh, Diego tried to find out more about Resh leadership.

The leaders weren't like kings, and they weren't elected like he heard some leaders were. The Resh world was divided into segments called yanoms, each governed by a group of leaders called 'yan' that were all in the same family. They were beholden to a world leadership called the yanomish. Several Resh were part of the yanomish, taking turns at being the head Yan. It confused him, but Diego pursued it further, requesting pictures of the yanomish.

The pictures were blurred as though the person taking it had done it covertly. Diego asked for clarification. He knew the computers sometimes could make sense of difficult-to-see pictures. The computer could only sharpen the photos a little, but it was enough. When he saw the yan, he gasped. That was the Resh in charge of the three who had interrogated them. There was a supposed name — Yan Win. But Win in the Resh language also meant "one." It was higher than one, but he would not try to figure that out either. Diego gazed harder at the others and realized they, too, were the same Resh who had been with Yan Win.

So, where had they been taken after their kidnapping from Grrlock? The cell he had awakened in didn't have the feel of something near water, and any building on the main island was near water.

"Commander, there is a military outpost on one of the dwarf planets."

Bress's information came up on his screen, and Diego studied all the details. It was a flat-sided minor planet, as rocky and desolate as the moon near his world but a great deal smaller. Like the other dwarf planets, it tumbled and rolled around the others as though they were trying to play catch with one another. It would be difficult to land on. However, that would make sense as a place for the Resh to take them as opposed to the primary world. He tried to remember his time with the Resh. Less gravity? Yes.

Bress stood in front of him. "Commander, we could land there, but we need to figure out the defenses. I need to see what happened to you when you were kidnapped to find any clues to help us."

Diego didn't enjoy opening his mind to others, even

though he trusted the Turengens. Here, he had no choice. "Yes, we need all the information we can get."

Think. Think! Think. Think. Think…

They were all taking part. So, Diego leaned back, closed his eyes, and tried to remember the moment after he woke up in the cell.

CHAPTER TWENTY-ONE

Diego didn't fall asleep, but this was the most relaxed he had been since this mess with the Resh began. He saw things from his kidnapping he hadn't remembered the first time. There were no Resh on Grrlock, so several Grrlocks carried out the actual abduction. He glimpsed one carrying Rrishan down the mountain, and then he saw a waiting ground transport. Diego felt a hard chair, then the pain from a quick and hard take-off, then floating, and finally, blackness.

The next thing he remembered was a landing—he felt gravity, but not Seressin one norm. Diego felt himself dragged down a cold metal corridor. No light against his eyelids. Then he was in the cell. He opened his eyes, looking for his companions, but saw Bress staring at him.

"A small asteroid. Not the Resh home world," the Turengen said. "In that, we are luckier."

"We need all the luck we can get," Diego muttered. "Could you tell which asteroid it was?"

Diego's computer was still up. The monitor showed the three asteroids, and Bress pointed to the one with a half-moon shape. He typed in a quick command, and the dead world magnified so he could see craters. There was a stark demarcation between the sun-drenched part of the world and the dark. Diego typed in more commands, and the world began revolving, showing him all areas, and giving many facts and details.

When the computer showed the flat side, Diego saw innumerable pockmarks and dark holes. "Landing bays," he murmured.

As though on cue, a small ship zipped out of a landing bay. It swung around the planet once, and then it headed toward the Resh home world.

"So, right now, all we have to do is to figure out how to sneak in there, find Rrishan and Fress, and sneak away." Diego gave a soft snort. Despite his optimism at having a site more accessible, it was still an almost impossible task.

"No. It is possible. I am working on electronic disguising of the ship," Krim interjected. "If it works, we will show up on the Resh computers as a supply ship. They wouldn't realize what we really are until they walk up to our ship."

This was beyond what Diego had hoped for. "How close are you to having something?"

"Cannot say, Commander. I am experimenting. I have never done this before."

"I will help, Commander," Bress began. "If you so order."

Diego hesitated, not wanting to drag his colleagues into a death trap.

"We do this because the Resh have one of our cousins and because we are following you," Bress declared.

With that announcement, the Turengen put their heads together, literally, and worked to solve the problem. Diego felt as though he was an unnecessary cog in this part of the wheel. He continued to study the information about the Resh outpost and the entire Resh system.

By the time Bress announced the passageway wormhole, Krim called out. "I think I have a disguise. Makes us look like a Quexling freighter."

Diego remembered his lessons. Quexling freighters carried luxury items and were slow. Krim had picked out the perfect bait. "We're going to see soon enough," Diego replied. "Go on through as we already planned, Bress."

"Yes, sir."

Even though there would not be a change in gravity or speed, Diego gripped the arms of the command chair in anticipation. He prayed nothing was waiting for them on the other side.

He felt a soft shaking and then a jerk.

"Resh system sun. Veering away," Bress announced.

Sweat trickled down his back. The monitor shaded the great red sun but couldn't keep out all of the heat. The air grew stifling. The gauge showed a rise in temperature, and then it lowered again. The ship's life support controls could finally cool the room down.

"I am tracking a ship going to the outpost. Only a small crew," Jeng reported.

"Like us?" Diego asked.

"Fewer. Three Resh. Must be a supply ship from the home planet."

"Monitor and see what the protocol is."

"Yes, Commander." Jeng made a soft chittering and gazed at the monitors in front of her with rapt attention.

"Krim, you monitor, too. See if there is any unusual reaction to our presence."

"Yes, sir."

Diego viewed the command chair monitor but knew the Turengen, understanding the technology better than he did, picked up more. He kept quiet and watched, listening for the translation of the transmissions. To his disgust, there wasn't much transmission, and part of it was garbled. The ship was delivering the things necessary for the visit of Resh dignitaries, but that was all he could pick up. "Does anyone know the Resh language at all?"

He heard five nos.

"That's our biggest problem. Still, we don't need to wait

for another ship. We need to go in soon," Diego mused aloud. "Krim, can they pick us out with their instruments?"

"Probably pick up basics – size, how many of us."

"Will they be able to tell you are Turengen and I am human?"

"Not you, but us – yes. Mainly because of our size."

"Could you make a disguise for each of us to show up on their screens as something different? Or just hide our sizes?"

"No, not now. We can send a signal, so things are hard to read."

"Sounds good, and when we get close enough, I'll do all the talking."

"Keep the ship disguise all the way in, Commander?" Krim asked. Her eyes sparkled. Diego thought she was enjoying this.

"Yes, if you can."

"I can."

"*Bueno*," he murmured. "Let's go in then."

"They are wondering about us," Bress said. Then he chittered. "That other ship – the one that was in the Grrlock system is heading there as well."

"Slow. Let them get there first," Diego instructed. He preferred not to have to deal with that kind of unknown in space. In fact, he'd prefer not to have any kind of confrontation at all. Then, he wondered if his idea was too simple and, therefore, doomed to failure.

Bress shook his head. "Simple might work where complicated wouldn't. Things on the ships get too complicated."

Diego just nodded, reading the stats Krim had sent to his monitors. It was an engine using spiral energy. Could that be a disguise, too? He watched as the monitor showed the other ship entering the planetoid's bay.

"Take us in slowly. Let me know if they make any offensive maneuvers." Diego took a deep breath. "Shish, when they try to contact us, open the communications so I can talk to them."

She gazed at him but turned back to her console with a nod. The ship continued at quarter light-speed, the asteroid increasing in size. Finally, there was a harsh croaking on the communications monitor. Diego heard only enough to understand the Resh were demanding to know who they were.

Now was the time to fool their enemy. Diego opened the communications control on his command chair, cleared his throat, and said in Spanish, "*This is the commander of the San Juan Batista. We sailed from California with treasure and information for the Resh Yan Win. We request landing privileges.*"

There was silence on the other end. Diego knew they understood his words about their leader, but the rest should be incomprehensible, at least until their translator could decipher Spanish.

Again, the Resh demanded to know who they were. Again, Diego repeated his request, even as they continued approaching the outpost. Several small ships sped from the bay toward them.

"Keep the shields up, but don't power the weapons."

"If we do that, then the disguise will not work," Krim said.

"All right, be ready to pull up the shields if they get hostile."

"Yes, Commander."

The small fighters drew closer.

CHAPTER TWENTY-TWO

The communicator continued blaring Resh at them, demanding to know who they were. Then, it changed to simple instructions for entering their bay. Even he could understand those. Diego smiled softly and motioned for Bress to continue. Apparently, the Resh were a little curious. He thanked them in flowery Spanish. The small ships escorted their cruiser into a gaping bay, and a bank of pulsing lights told them where to land.

After powering down the engines, Bress asked the obvious. "What do we do now, Commander?"

"What weapons do we have? Any sleep gas bombs?"

Jeng nodded and scurried to the arms locker.

"Krim, do you still have the disguise up?"

"No, Commander, not enough power."

Even as she spoke, a dozen Resh guards marched up to their ship and surrounded it.

"Prill, you take some of those bombs, too. Don masks. Let's see if our luck continues," Diego said.

"There are enough devices here," Bress began with a grin. "To knock out everyone in the entire bay, maybe even the base."

Diego nodded as he donned his small mask and gathered a half dozen of the bombs in his arms. The other Turengen did the same, placing their weapons in pouches hanging around their waists.

Punching the codes into the inner hatch, they waited as the

door cycled open. After they stepped through, it closed behind them. Diego pushed the outer hatch button. The group hugged the inside walls of the small chamber. He decided he was crazy, but they were here, so they had to follow through.

They swiftly discarded the bombs as soon as there was an opening. Popping noises like firecrackers told him the devices were deploying. The Turengen scattered through the partially open hatch, and Diego rushed forward as a Resh tossed something through the hatch. As he leaped into the bay, a booming roar threw him even farther. His knees hit the deck first, sending shockwaves up through his body.

Diego crawled forward, trying to peer through the smoke and haze. He glimpsed Bress and the others ahead of him. Stumbling to his feet, he caught up with them.

"I doubt we're leaving the same way we came," Jeng commented.

Diego looked over his shoulder and saw the mangled ruins of the outer hatch. He glanced around and, through the haze, saw several other small ships. First, Rrishan and Fress, and then they would steal a ship.

Diego threw himself to the ground when he saw several flashes from the other side of the bay. One flash came close enough for him to feel the heat from the weapon. He crawled through the haze, keeping equipment between him and the Resh. A similar flash from his right told him at least one of the Turengen had survived the onslaught. He had one more of the gas grenades. Half rising, Diego lobbed it toward the Resh. It popped, and the thick haze thickened. Most of the flashes stopped, but some of the toad-men were prepared for the gas and continued firing on them.

Diego pulled out a small laser pistol and tried to crawl closer. The charge might reach the soldiers but wouldn't do them any harm with their heavy body armor. A more powerful blast hit the object he was hiding behind, and he felt it shudder. Diego dashed to another shadowy object and realized it was a one-man delivery cart carrying supplies inside the spaceships. Still crouched, he slid into what he figured was a driver's seat and searched for a way to make it run. Pushing the floor with his foot made it move forward at a crawl, and Diego opted for that rather than wasting time trying to figure out the starting mechanism.

Despite being slow, it allowed him protection from the two or three Resh still fighting. He heard a screech and leaped out of the vehicle. One of the Turengen had been hurt. Something sizzled above his head, and he ducked even lower as he tried to run toward the otter-man. Weapons spat on both sides, but finally, the shooting stilled, and it grew quiet.

Diego reached the other side of the bay, where he found the five Turengen. Jeng looked a bit singed but not badly hurt. Several Resh lay still on the deck.

"Most are knocked out with gas," Krim said. "What do we do with them?"

"How long will they be out?" Diego asked.

"Not long. The gas is clearing out now," Bress explained.

"If we can find a room to lock them in…" Diego suggested.

It didn't take the Turengen long to find a storage room that would hold the seven unconscious Resh. They dragged them in and fixed the locking mechanism to keep them there.

"I'm surprised no one else showed up," Diego said.

"Been listening," Bress answered. "They are busy with something. Not sure what."

"Well, let's find Fress and Rrishan and get out of here," Diego stated. "Can you feel Fress?"

Jeng shook her head.

Prill looked thoughtful. "I feel something—different."

"What's different about it? Can you figure out where it's coming from?"

"I'm not sure, Commander." Prill's eyes widened. "Yes, I think I know where our kin is. There are Resh with them, though."

Diego frowned. "Can't help that. We'll have to deal with it when we get there."

"The Yan Win."

"We'll still have to deal with it when we get there," Diego responded. He felt the ominous tendrils of his dream. "We need to hurry as soon as we know the route."

"Most of it was in your head, Commander," Bress assured him. He pattered down a corridor, and the others followed close behind.

Diego felt anxious about an ambush, although he knew the Turengen could detect anyone trying that. He almost plowed into Jeng, who had stopped short. "What's the matter?" he whispered.

"A blankness ahead," Prill chittered softly back.

"Blankness?"

"No thoughts, nothing. Different from someone not being there."

"Like someone can disguise their thoughts?" Diego asked.

"Have heard of such, but rare," Bress added.

"Then I will see what's there."

"Commander," Jeng chittered. "I will go with you. Need someone small to help."

Diego nodded and crept forward, staying close to the wall. He chafed at the slowness of their progress, but if someone was out there…. He saw the movement of shadow around the bend and motioned to Jeng. She nodded and dropped to all fours. A gas grenade rolled along the deck and around the corner. A soft pop and tendrils of bluish-purple smoke drifted toward them.

An angry roar shook the walls as a massive Resh warrior stomp-hopped toward them. Another one thundered behind him. They had helmets Diego had not seen before and were wearing heavy body armor. Diego could only guess these strange helmets might be the reason the Turengen couldn't pick up their thoughts.

All six of Diego's group fired, concentrating on the most

vulnerable spots. Most of his pistol's charge was gone by the time the two Resh lay on the ground.

With a sigh, he motioned them to gather the Resh weapons and continue. It seemed interminable, but finally, they reached a corridor where Resh stood guard outside an immense door. Diego remembered being here and knew this was the audience chamber. *Do you think the gas bombs will take them out? Do you have any left?*

Yes. Three of the otter people activated and tossed the bombs in front of the guards. There was a pop, and the Resh wilted to the ground. It seemed too easy to Diego. He gazed at his troops in silent consultation. He pointed up, but Bress shook his head.

We don't know if they have emergency access tunnels, but these guards are not unconscious, only pretending.

With a shrug, Diego pulled one of the Resh weapons out of his belt and hoped he was changing the setting to stun. Then he dashed toward the guards. The guard rolled over as Diego fired. The Turengen did the same and neutralized the other two guards. Diego still felt it was too simple, but they had no choice. He gathered one of the guard's weapons and stuck it in his belt. Then he reached for the round door control. The others were ready with their confiscated arms.

CHAPTER TWENTY-THREE

The door slid open, and Diego saw the same Resh he had seen when he was a prisoner. Rrishan and Fress stood behind a glowing light, not ten feet in front of them. Then he saw they weren't moving. They looked like statues frozen in place.

"You have returned...." The Yan Win didn't finish his comment.

Diego and the Turengen tossed the remainder of their gas bombs and started firing at any Resh in the room. The three yan seemed to be protected by some kind of personal shield, as were several guards. Diego and the others dodged enemy fire, grateful for the gas bomb smoke floating up from the ground. They finally subdued the last guard by combining their stun weapons, but the Resh leaders remained still safe behind their personal shields.

"Let's get what we came for," Diego ordered while he grabbed another Resh weapon and held it on the three Resh leaders.

Yan Win screamed and croaked what Diego assumed were curses and threats. He didn't have time to deal with it. Escaping was the only object. He dashed to the glow still holding Rrishan and Fress, and then stopped short. He didn't know what it would do to him. The Turengen evidently didn't know either.

Diego sucked in a deep breath and stepped into the glow. His legs lost their power, and he fell, but he was still conscious. At least, he thought he was. Tingling rose from his legs into his body. His hands shook, but he felt strength in his legs again, and Diego rose slowly from the ground. The glow had disappeared, and the two prisoners lay on the ground. Diego grabbed Rrishan and threw her over his shoulder. Prill grunted as he picked up Fress and carried her on his back. Diego sprinted out of the audience room and into the corridor. The others followed. Fress was almost as large as Prill, but he still dogged Diego's heels.

"You going to make it?" Diego asked.

"Will make it," the otter man gasped.

They met no one until they were near the bay. A Resh guard leaned against the corridor wall, his weapon held loosely in his stubby hand.

"Wounded," Bress announced.

"You're hurt," Diego called out. "We won't hurt you if you don't try to stop us."

"Dead either way," the Resh croaked. "Will stop you." He jerked up his pistol with more speed than Diego thought he had.

But Diego was faster. He fired, hitting the Resh's lower leg. With a scream, the guard dropped to the deck.

Jeng ran up and grabbed the weapon. "You were brave, but we won."

The Resh groaned as the group ran past him and into the bay. There were no more guards. Diego couldn't believe there were only a few guards for such an important Resh. He heard banging and muffled voices from the room they had locked the other guards in, but keeping only a couple dozen on the whole planetoid seemed stupid to him.

"Check out our spaceship," Diego ordered, panting from carrying the extra weight.

"Why don't we take that ship?"

Diego's gaze followed where Bress pointed. It was the Resh ship with the revolutionary engine. "Remember the Koressian ground vehicle? It wouldn't run for anyone else except a Koressian. We don't have time to see if we can steal it. We have to take our own ship if we can. Check and see if there is integrity in the systems — engine room, control room, hull, and life support."

Diego thought as the Turengen scurried to follow his orders. Could they grab the computer specifications for the Resh ship? Disable it so that it couldn't follow. "Bress! Is there a way to get information about that ship's engine? And could it be disabled?"

Bress called Jeng, and they scurried to the other ship. Diego deposited Rrishan in a chair. She groaned as he snapped the restraints in place. Trill lay Fress on the deck, and he sagged down beside her, panting heavily.

Diego sat down in the command chair and powered up all the systems monitors. The engine room had not been damaged. Hull integrity proved to be good except at the hatch, but the inner hatch had not been compromised, and it would hold. The ship wouldn't be able to maintain top speeds, but all they needed was to reach a passage gate. He powered up the engines, weapons, and navigation, ready for the rest of the crew.

"What? What happened?" Rrishan choked out. Then she moaned and reached for the strap buckles.

"Leave them fastened," Diego ordered. "We're going to take off soon."

Krim trotted into the room, holding up a circular information disk. "Got it. Others coming."

"Bress, where's Jeng?"

"Setting a device," he chittered.

The cycling of the hatch told him she was on board. She reassured him telepathically.

"Help Prill with Fress. Everyone needs to be strapped in. Begin escape sequence," he ordered.

Jeng clattered into the room and threw herself into the navigation chair. "We need to go now," she panted.

"Take us out. As soon as we're clear, go into the fastest speed the ship can tolerate."

"Engines ready, and so are we," Bress declared. "Now!"

The ship lifted about a meter off the deck and then shot forward toward the bay opening. Diego expected it to close, but to his surprise, it didn't. "More speed!" he cried as they shot into space.

The Turengen got more speed. Gravity pushed Diego further into his seat, and he could hear the engines straining. Then, on the monitors, he saw a section of the irregularly shaped planet blowing out into space. What had once been an oval opening large enough to accommodate a medium-sized spaceship was now a gaping hole.

"What's going on?" Rrishan gasped. She was wide awake, her golden eyes staring at the main monitor. Diego couldn't tell if she was in pain, but there would be nothing they could do about it until they were out of the reach of the Resh.

The Turengen cheered their minor victory. No one would follow them out of that bay.

"Keep this speed as long as you can. Bress, is there a nearer gate than the one we came through? I don't want to test our damage against the Resh sun."

Bress studied his panel. "Yes, one in the same direction we are going, but a little closer to the Resh home planet."

Diego frowned. There was no help for it. "Whose territory is on the other side of the gate?"

"Most likely, Resh, but I am checking."

Diego studied his computer as well and found that the gate in question would take them to a small and undeveloped system. More luck, he hoped. Beyond that was a system both the Resh and the Seressins claimed. It had a planet that supported humanoids. Still, what he wanted was a way back to the Seressin home planet. He had done what he promised to do and would go back to report.

"The second gate leads to a disputed area, and the next is a Seressin system. Several more after that, take us to Seressin."

Bress answered Diego's unspoken question.

"Let's go that way and hope there's no interference on our journey."

Thankfully, the trip out of the Resh system was much smoother than Diego expected. It would seem the Resh were more worried about their leaders than catching a damaged ship heading out of the system. "Be ready for evasive action on the other side of the passage." He gazed at his monitor. Another hour.

He unbuckled and walked over to Rrishan's chair. She was wide awake by now but still not saying anything. "Are you all right? Did they do anything to you?"

She shook her head. "Kept us in that dark hole the whole time, then brought us out and told us about you, Rreengrol, and Hreeshan being traitors. And how you had destroyed the supreme commander."

"Your brother and Commander Hreeshan were mind-altered to destroy Commander Ziron's ship along with the supreme commander. I was told to work with them, or they would kill you and Fress. The Turengen blocked that plot, but the *Star Devourer* exploded, anyway." He sighed. "So, I vowed to come and get you and Fress or die trying. What's left of the crew agreed to join me."

Her golden eyes filled with tears. "So Rreengrol is dead?"

Diego nodded. "I'm sorry."

Several tears tracked down her cheeks and dripped from her whiskers. Then she blinked back more tears and shook her head. "I figured he had to be when they told me what you, Rreengrol, and Hreeshan had done. Fress figured all her kin were dead. We cried a lot. There is no more crying." She bared her teeth. "What happens now?"

"We try to get back to the Seressin home world and report."

"Good luck. The Resh brought us out to gloat before they killed us. They won't let this go."

"I know. That's why we're not wasting any time getting out of here. I also want to report to Grrlock and have those traitors arrested before they can do anything to your family. In the meantime, do you want to join my crew? They know more than their commander does."

She growled, her whiskers quivering. "Yes! I want to take care of Resh."

"Right now, we're trying to avoid them, but join Jeng on navigation," Bress suggested. "Best place with her abilities."

"Yes, a good choice," Diego concurred. "How close to the gate?"

"Soon," came the vague answer.

"How is Fress?"

"Still unconscious but doesn't seem to be hurt," Krim replied.

"Weapons ready, but go through with shields up." Diego glanced at the read-outs. "Or whatever shields are operative."

"Yes, sir."

"Are all the weaponry stations manned?" Diego asked.

"No. Aft isn't."

Diego unbuckled and took the aft station. Looking through the lens, the viewport showed him a little damage from the blown outer hatch.

"Going through," Bress announced.

Diego braced for the passage and felt the subtle 'pulling' of his insides and the shifting back to normal. In the monitor, two smallish fighters waited for them.

"Shields down!" Diego shouted.

Prill fired at the nearest one almost before Krim had lowered the shields. The ship blossomed into a silent inferno. Diego tried to get the other one in his sights, but it sped ahead rather than behind. Prill continued to fire, hitting it with a glancing blow. The ship fell away and behind. Diego took a breath and fired, also a glancing blow. The ship was no longer a threat, more seriously damaged than they were.

"Do you want us to finish it off, Commander?" Bress asked.

That would be the safest thing to do, but.... "No, shields up, and let's get to the other gate. And yes, I realize they could still have communications."

"Understood," Bress said, although he sounded disappointed.

Diego hoped his decision would not come back to exact retribution on them. "Shields up. Top speed."

The computers had been right. This was a dead system. Its star was a small white dwarf flickering in the distance. They dodged chunks of space debris, making Diego wonder if this had ever been an organized system. However, that was nothing to concern him right now. They were one system away from being back in Seressin territory.

"Any other ships?"

"Monitors picking up standard space debris, Commander."

"Which could hide ships."

"Maybe, but our sensors are pretty sensitive to the difference between rock and mechanical."

Still, Diego had a funny feeling as they approached the next gate. The chunks were larger than mountains, and the hills and mountains of his home planet could hide a great deal. He knew the analogy was not quite the same, but still....

"Approaching the passage gate to the Nuriss System. There may be a Seressin scout craft waiting there."

They approached the passage in silence. The others had most likely picked up on his mood.

"Prepare for trans..." Jeng didn't finish. Something boomed and shook the craft.

"Resh?" Diego called. He looked in his weapon's viewscreen and saw a craft streaking toward them. It fired at them. When it drew into range, he lowered the aft shield and fired. Once, then twice. The ship disintegrated.

Their ship continued to shake; claxons blared. "Damage report!" he shouted.

CHAPTER TWENTY-FOUR

They sped through the gate before anyone could say anything. More sirens blared as they emerged into the Nuriss System.

"We won't make it to the next gate, Commander!" Bress called. "Breach in life support, loss of hull integrity aft."

"Get into your enviro suits," Diego ordered. "Jeng, nearest habitable planet?" His ears popped. He took a deep breath, but it didn't satisfy his lungs.

"Your enviro suit, Commander." Bress held out one of the survival outfits. In his suit, the otter-man looked like a ball with a smaller ball on top.

Diego took his environmental outfit and slipped it on, glancing around at his crew. Everyone else had suited up. He sealed the headgear and heard Jeng's voice in his ears. "Fourth planet, Nurisna."

"Can we make it?"

"Yes, Commander, but it will be a hard landing. " No stabilizers."

"And if we're lucky and there are no other surprises," Bress added.

Diego couldn't help grinning. "All possible speed. And Krim, I'd like you to send a message to the Seressin home world."

"Best way is message drone."

"As we get closer to Nurisna, do it."

"Yes, sir."

"And shut off those sirens!" The noise immediately ceased. Diego stayed at the aft weaponry but still kept up with their progress on the aft computer. They were losing air as well as thrust. Still, the ship was maintaining the course. Diego suspected most of that was because of Bress's skill on the navigational computer. If they ever made it to Nurisna, it would be by the Turengen's skill and by heavenly help, Diego thought.

The fourth planet drew closer and closer, and Diego thought they might have some of that luck Bress had mentioned.

"Another ship has come through the passage gate," Jeng announced.

"When are the fish going to jump in our net?" Rrishan snapped.

Diego figured it to be some kind of Grrlock idiom, but there wasn't time for that now. "Can we beat him to the planet?"

"It'll be close, Commander. The Resh are doing near light speed while we can barely do quarter. And continuing to lose power."

"If you can, get more speed out of the ship."

"We have to save enough for a landing we can survive," Bress pointed out.

Diego studied the aft weaponry and noticed something interesting. "Ready for aft torpedo release?"

Bress chittered something, his voice emitting surprise.

"Lighten the ship," Diego explained tersely as he set the coordinates. "I don't think it will cause any damage, but maybe it will slow the Resh down." Diego couldn't agonize over his calculations. "Here goes the first one." He punched the button and felt the slight shudder of the weapon release. "Second one and the third one."

The ship seemed to lurch forward, but their speed didn't change. They continued toward the planet while watching the pursuing Resh ship gaining on them. Suddenly, the three torpedoes exploded in a single flash. The ship behind them spiraled out of range, then settled back to swift pursuit.

"It caused them a brief delay, Diego, er, Commander," Rrishan declared.

"Diego is fine. I am not a commander."

"Yes, you are," the Grrlock continued. "You got me out of that nasty pit!" She lowered her voice. "I never was afraid of the dark before this, but I was beginning to be in that Resh den. It was horrible."

Diego nodded, then turned back to his monitor. "Bress, can you tell me about this planet?"

"Nurisna is a planet well within survival range for us. It has an oxygen, nitrogen, and carbon dioxide mix that will allow us to move around without re-breathers. The terrain has some mountains but mostly hills and flatlands. It has a variety of plant growth and animal life. In short, we can exist there and wait for rescue without undue hardship, Commander."

Or recapture, Diego thought. From Bress's report, Nurisna sounded much like his homeland. "Plenty of water?"

"Intermittent lakes and rivers of varying sizes." Bress grinned. "Good to swim in."

Moaning came from Fress's chair. Krim hopped over to check on her. The Turengen took her gloved hand and gazed into Fress's eyes. Krim had to be using telepathy. Finally, Fress sat up.

"She knows the situation?" Diego asked.

"Yes, Commander."

"Hang on, Fress."

Despite their decreased speed, the ship sped toward the planet. Luck was in their favor, insomuch that the planet's orbit was on their side of the bright orange sun. The monitor showed him a whitish-yellow cloud covering. Then Diego saw breaks in the clouds where brown mingled with green, speckled with dots of blue green. Inviting, he thought.

Life support continued to leak out, and a new claxon blared. Hull integrity, Diego noted.

"Resh closing, sir. Soon, they will fire on us. Aft shields are inoperative," Krim reported.

Diego remembered what he had learned from Anaar, the android tutor. "Can we jettison the emergency pods?"

Bress blinked in surprise. "Yes! On your orders, Commander."

"Will it work in the upper atmosphere?"

"Rough, but yes."

Diego tried to do some quick figures but knew the Turengen were faster. "How close will the other ship be when we reach Nurisna?" He returned to the command chair, the aft weaponry useless.

"Too close, but...."

"Good. Be ready, crew. We are approaching the outer atmosphere. Send out the drone!"

There was a small thump. "Message sent," Jeng announced.

"Ready to jettison," Bress announced.

"Ready," Krim echoed.

Bumping told Diego they were arriving. "How close are the Resh?"

Something blazed past the viewport. Too close.

"Jettison!" Diego shouted. He heard grinding that hurt his ears, and the ship jerked sideways, then forward as the thrusters engaged.

"Going down steeply," Jeng announced.

Diego watched the monitors and saw the Resh ship firing on the emergency pods. They split into several large pieces, one of which careened toward the battlecruiser. He saw the ship trying to swing out of its way, but the upper atmosphere made the effort sluggish. The chunk of debris hit the back end of the Resh ship, and a flash told Diego it was a good hit. The Resh spun back out to space, seemingly out of control. "Take us down. If you can, find something with plenty of food and shelter."

"Large lake near forest area and hills," Bress announced.

"Which will be good because we can only make one try."

The ship bucked and rolled as though emphasizing the fact. Diego's stomach tired of it and was letting his head know. Gravity intensified. The ship bucked again. It was like a wild mustang refusing to give up its fight.

The ground came at them fast. Forward rockets slowed them down, but not enough for a controlled landing.

"Hang on. No workable landing gear," Bress called out, his voice shaky.

Diego hung on, the chair's safety apparatus reaching out to enfold him. The suit, the safety net, and the ground closing in choked him. The rockets fired again, struggling to slow them down. Then they hit and skidded, with metal buckling and screeching until blackness closed in.

CHAPTER TWENTY-FIVE

Commander? Commander!

The voice was incessant and annoying. Diego's head hurt. Everything hurt. He cracked his eyes open and saw—nothing! No, there was a bit of reddish light from behind him. It gave everything a hellish glow.

"Commander?" A whiskery face thrust itself close to his face. A Turengen. Bress. Small wisps of light-colored vapor rose to the ceiling. Some of it drifted toward him, and he coughed. That made his head throb.

"Casualties?" he choked out. Then he realized his helmet was gone. *Of course, you're choking on the smell of burning wires.*

"No one dead; no one badly hurt. Bumps, bruises, sprains as far as we can tell, Commander," Jeng said. "We should leave. In case…."

"Check the exit hatch. Blow it if it doesn't open with controls."

"It has a mechanism to do that," Prill informed him.

"All right. Gather everything usable. Any rations, weapons, medical supplies," Diego ordered.

"Not much left in the ship," Rrishan pointed out.

"Probably more than we think," Diego replied, slowly getting to his feet. His legs held him up. He sighed in relief. All of his body parts seemed to be intact.

The ship, or what the crash left of it, slanted just enough to make walking difficult. He held on to the console, another chair, and made his way to a wall near where the science and computer stations once stood. Placing his hand on the doorplate, Diego tried to get the panel to open. It grated, gave a loud screech, and then stopped. "Bring over something to pry this open."

Rrishan brought a broken rod and shoved it in the crack. Together, they pushed and then pulled. The panel opened a little more.

"If we try again, I'm sure we can get in," Krim said.

Diego and Rrishan grunted with effort. He knew Grrlocks had a great deal of strength, but she had been in a cell for days, so he redoubled his efforts. With a groan, the metal pulled back some more, and Krim and Bress slipped in. The ship shuddered and slid sideways. Diego and Rrishan kept their grip on the rod, not wanting the door to slip back and trap the two Turengens.

Krim and Bress started pushing packages and boxes out the narrow opening. Diego didn't even look to see what was in them. If it was in the locker, then it was probably important for survival. Jeng passed each package to the crewmembers behind him as Diego and Rrishan continued to hold the door open. Sweat rolled in his eyes. There was a slight shudder, but the ship didn't slide anymore. It didn't take long for the two otter people to empty the locker. When they slipped out, Diego and Rrishan let go of the rod, and the door slid shut with a screech. He heard a harsh boom aft, indicating someone had blown the hatch.

"Everyone out. If you see something important, grab it, but don't go looking for things. At least not right now." He and Bress were the last to leave. *Anything else you would suggest salvaging?* he asked.

Bress gave a lopsided grin and shook his head. "Can come back tomorrow. Don't think the ship is going anywhere."

Diego could only laugh. "Do we have anything to signal any Seressin scouts if they come to investigate?"

Bress patted a device attached to a belt crossing over one

shoulder. The other belt carried small weaponry. "Only we have to be careful because it will also signal a Resh scout."

Diego sighed. "Let's see what this world looks like."

Bress said nothing, only pattered over to what remained of the aft hatch. The explosion had torn it off its hinges.

Diego was the last one out, but when he stepped out under the late afternoon sky, he gasped. It looked familiar and yet unfamiliar. In front of him, rolling grassland spread to the horizon. The waving grasses were a reddish-gold, seed-heads bowed as though ripe. When Diego observed further, he saw a dark, greenish band in the distance. He looked through his surveillance lenses and realized they were trees or some kind of tall growth. Lowering the lenses, he felt his heart thumping in time to imagine the hoofbeats of his long-dead friend, Tejas.

He had responsibilities, though. The similarity to his home world could only be on the surface. "Let's find a suitable camping place, something defensible."

"All this grassland could make that difficult," Rrishan commented.

"We'll make do," Diego replied. "I don't think the Resh will show up for a few days, and it will probably be twice that before we can expect anyone from Seress."

"We have protection from wild animals," Jeng added, pointing to a medium-sized package.

"A repelling device?" Diego asked.

Jeng nodded. "And several weapons."

"We'll be judicious with both," Diego instructed. "Let's try to make the terrain work for us before we advertise our presence with gadgets. Besides, we don't know how long we'll be here."

"This is like your home, Commander?" Bress asked.

"Yes."

"Good. You will know how to use this land for our advantage."

"But it's not my home." If the truth be told, Diego

expected to see a herd of cattle or horses racing over the nearest hill. Studying the area closest to them, he noticed several narrow trails of trodden down grasses. There were animals! "Keep a close watch for wild animals."

"How do you figure that, Commander?" Rrishan asked.

Diego just pointed to the flattened grasses. Then he started toward the crest of the nearest hill, leaving the technology to the others.

Rrishan caught up with him, as did Bress. "Your home was like this?"

"Some of it was. My father's hacienda was on land much like this." He really didn't want to talk about it right now. "Some of Grrlock resembled my home, too."

She nodded her head but said no more. Diego was grateful.

The grass reached waist high, and occasionally, out of the corner of his eyes, Diego thought he saw something scurrying along the ground through the growth. "Keep a watch. There are small animals living here. Hopefully, they aren't dangerous."

"A seed eater would love it out here," Rrishan added.

Bress had more of a problem pushing through the thick grass. "The grass is the perfect place to hide."

Rrishan looked at him in alarm. "Do you think something might be lying in wait?"

Diego shook his head. "Not something as large as we are."

"It's the slithering things I don't like."

Diego chuckled. "Snakes live in grasslands like this, but the snakes I am familiar with don't lie in wait for people to walk by." They reached the top of the hill. He surveyed the area without the lenses and then with. The wooded area looked ideal, but it would take them a while to reach it. Regardless of what lived in the forest, Diego felt they would be safer under cover. He looked for some kind of lake or river and didn't see one. There had to be some water source nearby to sustain all those trees. In the opposite direction, Diego saw clouds bunching on the horizon, building toward the sky like smoke from a fire. They started out fluffy and whitish pink. Then they grew darker, thicker, with bright flashes glowing inside. It was like the lightning was a prisoner inside the clouds. They grew so fast it alarmed him. "Come on. We need to get back to the group."

"Is that a storm?"

"Yes. I don't think I've seen one grow that large in so short a time."

They reached the rest of their group. "We need to shelter inside the ship temporarily." Diego told them what he and Rrishan had seen.

"It is coming our way, Commander," Bress added.

Clouds reached for the sky above the crest of the hill. The group trooped back into the ship.

"This will give us the opportunity to see if there is anything else salvageable," Prill said as they stowed their gear against the lower wall. By the time they were inside, the gust roared against the outer hull and sometimes forced a tendril of wind through the ruined hatch.

"Who's going to play cook?" Diego asked as the heavy gale rocked their ship.

"I will," Fress announced. She clambered over the pile until she found a box that held the emergency rations.

Diego sat in the command chair and brought up a monitor using the emergency battery. Outside, the grass swirled, alternately flattening to the ground and whipping around. The sky was a dark gray purple, almost black in places. Unidentified debris blew past the monitor's outer lens. Diego was relieved they had not tried getting to the woods right away. The ship wasn't space-worthy, but it was safe from a ground storm. At least, he hoped so. The rain wasn't the worst hazard. It was the wind. Another gust shook the ship and what came through the hatch had a bite of cold to it.

Rrishan and several of the Turengen tied down a couple

of blankets across the opening. That helped, but the temperature still dropped. The group finished their food and curled up in various corners to get some much-needed sleep. Fress offered to stay awake and monitor the one computer with power.

CHAPTER TWENTY-SIX

When Diego awoke, someone had pulled away the blankets from the hatch. Fress sat nearby with another emergency food pack. She held it out for him.

"Why didn't someone wake me up to pull guard duty?"

"You were tired. You are the commander. We took turns," Fress responded.

Diego frowned but didn't argue. The others had also gleaned while he slept, too. Someone pried open several other compartments. The backpacks didn't look bigger, so they must have divided everything equally. While he broke open one of the dry nutrition bars, Diego thought of what was ahead.

"It will take more than one day to reach the woods," Bress pointed out.

"I know, and we'll be in the open most of the way. Still, we can't stay here. It's the first place the Resh will look." Diego finished the protein bar and stood up to stretch. "The computer still working?"

"Yes, Commander," Bress replied.

"Bress, you are a sub-commander, too. We are marooned on this planet. We're all equal. Call me Diego, like you did before. You make me feel old."

Bress chittered his disapproval, but then he gave a knowing grin. "Will consider that an order. By the way, I checked. There aren't many dangerous predators, but there are a few."

"Let me look at the information, too." Diego was interested in seeing other similarities to his home planet.

"Good idea. When you are finished, I was going to pack the computer and an energy pack."

"You can do that?" Diego asked.

"Limited in what it can do, but it can give information already in data reservoir."

"I'll only be a few minutes."

"We will set up a triggering device while you search."

"Triggering?" Then he realized. "We'll know when someone is checking out the ship."

"Yes. And hopefully, we'll know if it's Seressin or Resh."

"Yes." Diego gazed at the vid-file on Nurisna, specifically on the flora and fauna. He had hoped to see something like horses, but the closest thing was long-legged, tall animals with ropey tails, cloven hooves, somewhat short necks, and horse-like heads. They had striped rumps, and their pelts were thick. There was the stump of a horn in the middle of its forehead. These were animals slightly resembling sheep or deer or buffaloes, especially if they had longer legs, bigger bodies, and brown wool.

"That is an unknown, Com…Diego."

He looked more at the ground wildlife. Diego didn't want anyone stepping on a snake or similar deadly animal. There were a variety of smaller creatures, some appearing to be candidates for hunting. The programmers conjectured that the seed-heads of the wild grasses were edible. Perhaps they could be ground into a type of flour to make tortillas if they were on Nurisna long enough. Various fruits grew in the forests. They wouldn't starve.

The dominant predator resembled a small mountain lion with a large head, muscular short body, and thickly furred tail. Studying the size of its paws, Diego figured this predator hunted more by ambush rather than speed. Such a creature would interest Rrishan and Rreengrol. Diego felt a pang of sadness when he thought of Rreengrol. He shut off the tutorial and helped Jeng unhook the monitor from the command chair. He stored it in his pack as it had the most room.

"How is it going, Bress?"

"Almost done. The detector cannot tell the difference in visitors, only that it has been visited by something other than an animal."

"That's better than nothing."

"Indeed." Soon, Bress had joined them on the prairie.

A moderate wind blew the grass, making it appear like waves in the ocean. They heard loud hooting somewhere in the distance, but the wind made it hard to tell which direction it came from.

"Let's see how far we can get." Despite their crash landing, harsh treatment by the Resh, and the destruction of the *Star Devourer*, Diego felt a strange excitement building inside. This was something he was familiar with.

Rrishan walked up beside him. "How is this the same as your world?"

"The hills, the wind."

"There are a few places like this on Grrlock. I like the mountains better, though."

"Your mountains are a great deal more rugged than the ones I am used to. Although I had been told about places on my world where mountains were tall."

"True. Worlds are big places. I suppose they can have many landscapes."

Diego nodded. "Although I read that most of Nurisna is like this. Mostly plain and rolling hills."

"Boring."

Diego laughed. "Probably not to those living on it."

"Do you think there are intelligent life forms living here?"

"Why not? Intelligent life forms come in all different shapes and sizes. Look at the Resh."

"You look at them. I'm not interested."

Diego laughed again but said nothing.

"Do you think Rreengrol is dead?" she asked again, her voice lowered to a whisper.

"The evidence points to it. I saw the blast of the *Star Devourer*."

"And he and Commander Hreeshan caused it."

"No!" Diego snapped. "The Resh caused it."

"You're right. The Resh did." They walked in silence for several minutes. "I still want to join the warrior forces."

"You will be a great warrior."

They continued walking in silence for some time. Diego glanced at the ground every few feet, knowing small creatures lived there. He had seen nothing on the computer about snakes, but that didn't mean none lived here. Mostly, he watched the forest ahead. The group walked to the top of a somewhat taller hill. The ship was still visible, but only barely. From here, Diego noticed small game trails through the thick grasses. As they continued, he assigned several of the crew to serve as lookouts. Diego knew the Turengens' telepathic abilities would overcome their physical handicap in the tall grass. Every few hours, they rotated jobs.

When the orange-colored sun was just past overhead, they found another rise and sat down to rest and eat some of the survival rations. It had grown hot, and tiny flying insects bit him. They flew around Rrishan and the Turengen as well, but their pelts were deterrents to insects.

"Will be glad to find a pond or river," Prill complained.

"So will I," Diego conceded. He hoped they would find both when they reached the woods. He slapped a large flying insect with an equally enormous appetite and then drank from his water bottle.

They continued through the afternoon. Diego was grateful to see they had gone more than half the distance from the ship to the forest by the time he called a halt to their day's trek. Again, they chose a taller hillock. This one had a stand of stunted trees halfway down the other side. Something made a trilling noise in a nearby tree. Diego would have said a bird, but he had seen enough in his recent past that he couldn't make such an assumption. At least it sounded happy. "Secure the perimeter of the camp with the repeller."

Jeng and Prill had the little box-like device set up in short order. As the orange sun turned blood red, the group ate their rations. The little blue lights on the force field box blinked in a steady cadence.

Diego munched on the protein sticks and realized he would be glad to do some hunting just to have a fresh dinner. He suspected the Turengen would do their own hunting once they found a lake or river. He never asked what their people preferred, but being aquatic, Diego assumed fish was part of their diet. Right now, even that would taste good.

After finishing the semi-sweet wafers that served as a dessert of sorts, Diego got up, dusted dirt off his pants, and walked down to the small trees. The creature had stopped its song when the force fields were set up but had not flown or leaped away. Now, he was curious. Fress joined him.

"The creature is still there," she informed him.

"I thought so. Can you tell what kind of animal it is?"

"No, and I cannot get anything from its mind. I suppose we annoyed it because we interrupted its hunting."

Diego slipped his hand into his pocket and felt the last wafer. He stopped just before the first tree and waited. A branch shivered and then shook as a fist-sized scaled creature leaped into the air. Diego noted it wasn't entirely scaled. The wings and back were covered in short feathers, while the head, belly, and chest had scales. It didn't have a beak but more of a long, pointed muzzle. It fluttered higher but didn't go away. Perhaps it felt the force shield and didn't want to try it further.

Diego broke the wafer in half and laid it on the branch

where the reptile-bird had perched. Then he backed away.

"Perhaps it will be a friend," Fress said, picking up on his thoughts.

"Yes, or another type of warning system." The creature was watching him, hovering, wings flared to catch the slight breeze. Diego didn't wait to see what the bird would do; they returned to camp. He sat gazing at the red sun almost below the far horizon.

"Should we build a fire?" Rrishan asked.

Diego shook his head. "In case the Resh arrive sooner than expected, we don't want to advertise our presence. Our sleeping gear should keep us warm enough."

The wind increased during the night, but they lay on the lee side of the hill, close together. Diego figured he was the only one suffering from the cold, but after he'd been in the sleeping bag for a while, he warmed up enough to fall asleep. The force shield box chirped like a baby bird in his ears.

Diego woke up before dawn to slight snores and heavy breathing telling him the others still slept. His breath formed clouds above his sleeping bag. Some bright stars winked, but the object most catching his attention was a smallish moon overhead. It shone blue green with dark blotches and two shining yellow spots resembling eyes. As he watched, a meteor shot across the sky, then several others.

Diego heard buzzing like insects. Further in the distance, he heard a kind of barking howl. He decided he could make himself useful by pulling out the breakfast rations. Diego frowned, realizing he would rather eat the porridge substance the cooks made on the *Star Devourer* than these survival rations. Still, they were keeping them alive, so he couldn't gripe.

He slid out of his sleeping bag, waking none of the Turengen, pulled on his cold weather jacket, and attached his personal weaponry to their various hidden and not hidden places. A clacking near their supplies had him pulling out his pistol and wishing for the night vision the Turengen seemed to have.

Diego crept closer and heard the clacking again. It sounded like something robotic, but he wasn't sure. One more step, more clacking. Diego flipped on the small artificial light. There was a flurry of clacking, and then the bird-reptile flew at him.

CHAPTER TWENTY-SEVEN

Diego fired his pistol, and the feathers and scales exploded in one last squawking clatter.

"What is it?" Fress dashed up, buckling on her bandoleer.

Diego crept closer, startled to see the creature was mechanical. Pieces of metal and plastic littered the area. A feather drifted down from the dark sky.

"Whose is it? Seressin or Resh?" the Turengen asked.

"I don't know, Fress. I've not been part of the Seressin Empire that long." Diego sighed. All their luck had been bad lately.

"It would be great if it was Seressin." Bress had already slipped on his backpack. He nudged a piece of metal with his paw. "But I haven't heard of anything like this among Seressin inventors."

Diego snorted. "You haven't been a big part of Seressin affairs either."

"That is true," Bress admitted.

He heard noises behind him, and Diego knew everyone was awake now. "We need to pack our gear and get out of here. We can eat as we walk. If this thing was Resh, then it would have heard a full evening of conversation and could have passed along our location. I'd rather be paranoid and apologize to a rescue party later than end up recaptured."

It didn't take long to gather up everything. The sun was just beginning to rise when the group set off on a narrow trail leading toward the forest.

As the sun rose, Diego pulled off his jacket and stuffed it into his backpack. Occasionally, he looked behind but saw nothing. He didn't hear any aircraft, either.

Halfway through the afternoon, the group reached a river. The water only reached Diego's knees, yet he estimated it to be at least twenty feet wide. Swift water splashed over rocks while slower eddies and deeper pools alternated. Diego sent two of the Turengen to look for a safer crossing.

Jeng grinned, pulled off her pack and bandoleer, and then dove in. Krim was right behind her. Diego followed their progress for a few minutes. They were like large bullets, darting here and there, and he knew they were enjoying themselves while they reconnoitered. He pulled out the long-range lenses and studied the far shore. There was a wide grassy area on the far shore before the beginnings of the forest. Diego couldn't see into the dim shadows between the trees.

Wait! Diego adjusted the lenses, changed the filter, and saw shadows flitting among the trees. A bipedal intelligent life-form or an animal, he asked himself. He continued looking but saw nothing else. He finally decided they would have to get across the river before he could find out.

"Jeng tells me there are creatures in the forest. She has felt their minds but can't make out what they are thinking," Bress told him.

Diego nodded. "I saw something over there, but it was just vague shapes. Regardless of what's over there, I think we need to get across before nightfall. Since Rrishan and I are taller, we can carry the more delicate equipment and the unpackaged food. Anything that can stand to get wet, your group will take. Have Fress and Jeng figured out the safest route across?"

"Yes, Diego," Bress replied. "We might make it in one trip.

There are waterproof coverings we can use to float over some of our supplies."

"Let's get it done then."

They quickly divided and packaged the supplies for the crossing. Diego pulled on his pack. The extra weight made his upper muscles creak, but it wasn't more than he could handle. Fress waded out into the river and then dived in. She resurfaced near the middle and stood on a big rock, gesturing the direction Diego and Rrishan should take. Diego went first.

As soon as he stepped foot in the shallow water, a chill seeped into his bones. Even through the waterproofed and insulated material of his boots, the flowing water was frigid. Nearby, in the deeper water, the Turengen swam easily, pushing their containers ahead of them. Diego envied their waterproof and warm pelts. Stepping into deeper water brought his mind back to his task. Water slopped over the top of his boot, and he shivered.

"You all right, Diego?" Rrishan asked. She followed him, carrying a pack every bit as heavy as his. She hissed as the water splashed on her.

"Yes, I just need to pay more attention to where I'm stepping and quit envying the Turengen. How are you doing?"

"Fine, although I don't like how parts of this river seem to race rather than flow."

"I agree. And we're coming up on one of them." Diego slowed a bit and gingerly stepped into a deeper section. The water pulled at his legs, but he maintained his balance.

By the time he and Rrishan reached the other side, the Turengen were on their way back for the few supplies they couldn't take the first trip. Despite the shallowness of the water they had waded through, Diego was exhausted. The backpack joined the other supplies Bress and his companions had ferried over. The sun was low on the horizon by now, beating on his back. Sweat trickled inside his tunic, and despite crossing a frigid river, he felt hot and itchy.

Rrishan lay her pack next to his. "It will be dark soon. Shouldn't we set up camp?"

"Yes," he said absently, gazing at the forest. He had the unshakable feeling they were being watched. Diego turned back to the Turengen, bringing the last of the supplies on shore.

Before Diego could say anything, Bress nodded, pointing toward the forest. "They are watching."

"I know everyone is tired, but let's get camp set up," Diego said. "Put out the force shields, but don't activate them until dark."

Everyone went to work with silent determination to get done so they could rest. As the sky darkened, Rrishan turned on a lantern, and Fress and Prill distributed the almost tasteless nutritional bars and water dispensers. Diego lay against the bole of a tree, hearing a variety of insect and animal noises. Despite knowing only a little about Nurisna, the noises soothed him, and he felt somewhat at peace. This could be a base of sorts where they could watch for Resh or Seressin, as well as reconnoiter. And he wanted to explore this world while he had a chance. Being a warrior was fine, but he missed interacting with the animals and those who took care of them. He missed Earth. Small lights flickered on and off in the forest like the fireflies he saw at various times of the year back home, and he got up to inspect them closer. Diego passed between two trees, then pulled out his hand-light.

He saw a shadow flitting between trees, then another. Leaning forward, he flicked on the light and saw a figure he had only seen on the *Star Devourer*—a Hoorinoo. Diego took one step toward the creature, and something grabbed his arm, something else covered his mouth, and yet something else pulled his legs out from under him. He kicked, but Diego felt woozy, things wavering in and out of his view. It was like a fog covering his mind, much like the time when the Koressians had slipped something in their dinner—back when the insect aliens were trying to kill his commanders.

The last thing he heard was the distant chittering of one of the Turengens and then nothing.

CHAPTER TWENTY-EIGHT

Dappled light filtered through heart-shaped leaves as Diego woke up. He tried to look around without moving his head, but that became impossible. A headache pounded inside his skull. How did he get to this place? There had been the shadowy figures — the creature that looked like Phris, his first teacher after his capture. The shadows had grabbed him before anyone could do or say anything. At night. Apparently, his captors had held him all night.

The shade under the trees provided refreshing coolness. Whatever lay underneath him was softer than anything he had slept on before. Diego turned his head and tried to see better that way. Everything was blurry, but then a figure came into greater focus. Was that Phris? No, this creature was bigger, almost shoulder height, but the resemblance was uncanny. The lavender fur, the large light blue eyes, and a round fishlike mouth. This wasn't Phris, but these creatures had to be Hoorinoo.

Diego smiled, but the round mouth didn't change at all. It stared down at him in an unchanging attitude. The large blue eyes blinked and continued gazing at him. Phris had never given him any of his people's words during that early time when they were together. The Seressin had forbidden it. So, there was nothing but Seressin to speak, or Grrlock, or Spanish. Diego was loath to start out with Seressin. Phris had been a slave like himself, so he figured these people wouldn't like Seressin. He motioned for permission to get up.

The lavender-downed man backed away a step and continued watching. Diego saw others farther back. Most of them carried staffs, or spears, or other primitive weapons. He sat up and then stood. In the distance, Diego could hear shouting. The creatures hooted to one another, telling him these creatures were related to Phris.

Until he could speak to them, he wouldn't know. He pointed, "Hoorinoo?"

The one closest to him moved closer and shook his spear, hooting and making other sounds.

Diego tried Grrlock. "I have a friend named Phris."

"You are Seressin!" The Hoorinoo seemed to speak Seressin very well.

"No," Diego replied. "I am a Seressin citizen, but I am human."

"Not a slave?"

"No. I earned my freedom, just as most of my companions did. Did the Seressin come here to get slaves?"

The Hoorinoo hooted. It was an angry sound. "Yes. Is that why you are here?"

"No," Diego replied. "While the Seressin came to my world for slaves, they are learning that having friends and allies is better than having slaves."

The hooting seemed more like laughter. "You earned your freedom, you said."

"Yes. Warrior training and then promotion during combat. I am a sub-commander."

The Hoorinoo poked Diego with his staff. Diego suddenly had it in his hands, swung it around, and laid the point on the lavender man's chest. The robin's egg eyes got even larger. Diego handed it back.

"Why are you here?"

"It's complicated. The Resh captured me and several of my

warrior companions and tried to get us to destroy the Seressin leaders. The Resh forced my warrior companions to destroy the Seressin leaders, but I wasn't affected. My Turengen crew and I went to the Resh home system to rescue two of our captured people. Our ship suffered damage and crashed on your planet when we escaped.

"The Resh come here more often than Seressin. Resh take slaves, too."

"Seems to be a bad habit around here, doesn't it?" Then Diego remembered some of his own people's habits. It didn't matter who did it. It was a despicable practice.

Several of the Hoorinoo hooted. Laughter erupted as they caught his sarcasm.

"Let us go to your comrades before they charge the forest. I do not think that would be a good idea," the Hoorinoo said. "I am Hriffin."

"Diego Perez. Most just call me Diego." He didn't ask about Hriffin's second sentence. He figured he'd find out soon enough.

"Dee-a-ya-go. Good."

Hriffin pronounced Diego's name just as Phris had done. He motioned them all on a dim, very narrow path leading through the forest.

The ground beneath Diego's feet was spongy but not wet. Animals chittered in the treetops, and some made clicking and clacking noises from the bushes. There were other noises sounding familiar to him, but they let him know just how far away from home he was. Diego didn't stray from the path, Hriffin's vague warning still in his mind. He brushed away the insects buzzing in front of his face and slapped whatever was biting the back of his neck. It didn't take long to reach the edge of the forest and the river. As they stepped out of the shadows, the Turengen and Rrishan formed a solid line, brandishing their weapons.

"Commander!" Bress cried, staring suspiciously at the

Hoorinoo.

For their part, the lavender people stood quietly, their weapons ready by their sides.

"Put your pistols away. They thought we might be slavers coming to get more captives. Apparently, this is a planet where the Resh and Seressin capture slaves. I knew one of their relatives on the *Star Devourer* right after my capture from my home planet." Diego turned to Hriffen. "There's something you might want to know."

The Hoorinoo waited as still as a tree trunk.

"Before we crashed on your planet, we sent off a small communications beacon. We don't know how long it will take to get through the star gates to Seressin or even if it will get there. We may be rescued, or we may be stranded."

Hriffen thumped his staff on the ground. "So be it. Whether you are here for a long time or a short time, you are welcome."

One of the other Hoorinoo had been surveying the group. "There are females among the warriors?"

"Yes," Diego replied. "If there is anything they cannot do, they haven't informed me of their limitations yet."

"Permission to speak freely, Commander?" Jeng asked, first looking at Diego and then turning to Hriffen.

"Yes."

"Sir, where are *your* females?"

Hriffen appeared ready to snap off an answer, and then he hooted with laughter. "Our females are strong and capable as well. There is a different reason they are not with us. We will discuss all and exchange ideas as we travel."

Diego grabbed his backpack from Krim and slipped it on.

The group didn't go through the forest as before but along the stream to a point where it bent toward the forest. There, a wider path opened under the trees. The Hoorinoo led them deeper and deeper into the woods.

After what seemed like a great deal of time, they stopped

to rest and eat. Diego slid off his heavy backpack and offered some of their nutrition bars to the Hoorinoo. They shook their heads and pulled out something that looked like small, round cakes. It wasn't long before they continued on the forest path. Shadows began darkening the trail, and Diego had to watch for things he might trip over. He heard hooting and singing ahead of them. Then, the distinct sound of a horse neighing.

Diego jerked at the noise. "What was that?"

CHAPTER TWENTY-NINE

"That is a reop," Hriffen said. "They live on the edges of the forests and on the plains. We use them to carry our supplies when we change camp locations."

"It sounds like an animal that lived on my world."

"Perhaps it will be similar."

"Perhaps." Diego was eager to meet this creature that sounded like animals he only dreamed about now. Soon, he saw flickering streams of light shining between the trees and heard melodic hooting. More voices joined in and became loud by the time they walked out of the woods and into the clearing.

A dozen houses met his gaze, squarish, and each built against a large-trunked tree. They were constructed from split wood, bark, and rushes, some tall enough to have a second story, as his hacienda back on Earth had. The Hoorinoo builders fastened the roofs to the trees, intertwining branches with thatch. Short stone walls served as footings at the base of the buildings. A few of these houses were quite large.

Well-clothed Hoorinoo greeted them, and Diego assumed these were the females. Only their eyes and mouths were showing. It reminded him of what he had heard the Moorish women did in southern Spain.

Beyond that, Diego saw several large, four-legged animals. Their limbs were long, and one of them dug up the soil with cloven hooves. The two in front hung their horse-shaped heads over a crudely built fence, showing short necks. The breeze ruffled long, ropy manes growing all the way down the back of their necks. Their swishing tails were also ropy, more like a cow's than a horse's. In fact, Diego thought, there was a bit more of the deer in the pedigree of the reop than there was of a horse, but he approached the nearest one. It gazed at him from the other side of the fence, flicking long, pointed ears. The eyes that studied him were more horse-like than anything else. The hide was short and tightly curled, mostly brown, but with a few dark stripes splashing across its rump. This was the creature he had seen on the computer, except less sheep-like.

"They bite," Hriffen warned him.

Bress walked to the paddock with him. "You used to ride something like this?"

Diego let a picture of his horse gallop through his thoughts.

"Oh," Bress said. "There are some differences."

Diego laughed. "Yes, there are." He stopped out of reach of the muzzle and teeth.

The reop leaned over the fence to smell him and Diego let it, not moving. No one else nearby moved either. Leathery lips nuzzled his clothes and moved up to smell his upper torso. Still, Diego didn't move. The reop smelled his face, and then its head flashed forward. The yellowish teeth snapped, but they clashed together on empty air. Diego had leaned back and then clapped his hand on the animal's nose. It jerked back, snorting, then reached forward again. This time, it didn't try to bite him. It only sniffed.

Diego reached up with his hand against the soft muzzle. It leaned over to bite again, but not with the force it had before. Diego pulled back at the last second and again laid his hand on the reop's nose.

"I have never seen one do that before," Hriffen said.

"I behaved differently."

"We keep them under control with a lip ring when we

need them to work."

Diego examined the bottom lip and saw where that would keep control. "May I try something with this one tomorrow?"

"Of course. It would be good to see another way of working with a reop."

"Thank you." Diego reached up and stroked the muzzle again. This time, the reop let him and Diego rubbed places that his gelding, Tejas, had liked. The animal seemed to like it, too, and snorted. After a while, it pulled back. Diego took in all of this one's differences, then saw a brand on the reop's rump. He memorized it, then spoke softly to the reop before he walked away. It snorted after him.

"Is that a male animal, Hriffen?"

Another Hoorinoo answered. "It is gelded."

Diego nodded. "Thank you. Is he yours?"

"No, they belong to the entire clan."

Everyone assembled in the center of the village, where someone laid out strange-colored stones in a circle. Most of the stones were opaque blue, yellow, and green, but there were a few red and purple ones as well. He wondered if they were there to sit on with their smooth, flat tops. If so, there was not enough. An old Hoorinoo female built a small fire in the middle of the circle as the sun set. Then Diego noticed how the flames were reflected in the depths of the stones. And not just reflected but amplified. To Diego's amazement, as the air cooled, he felt warmth emanating from the colored stones.

Fress dug out their rations while several of the females pulled out baskets and containers of local foods. Fress, Prill, and several Hoorinoo took the different foods and made an interesting and tasty dinner.

Diego enjoyed something that looked like sauce-covered twigs but tasted like crispy tortilla strips. There was a mashed mixture resembling corn porridge bursting with explosive spices in his mouth. As far as he could see or taste, there was no meat.

"I feel guilty that I didn't even know the eating habits of my first teacher, Phris," Diego said. "Are your people vegetarians?"

"Yes," Hriffen replied. "We gather the fruits and nuts off the forest trees and dig edible roots near rivers and streams. Occasionally, we will catch fish and eat those."

"Who is this Phris you have talked about?" one of the older females asked. She sat down next to Hriffen.

"He was my first teacher. Smaller than you, but otherwise exactly like your people. Phris helped me get used to the ship and learn the language and the customs of a battle cruiser. Where I came from, the most advanced type of transportation was a creature like the reop."

"Phris, in our language, means teacher," the female replied. "And if he was smaller, he could have still been in the young stage. Or he could have stopped his growth. Our people can do that if they feel the need."

Diego wanted to ask more about it but, for some inexplicable reason, felt this wasn't the time. "Since I got my freedom, I wanted to find out how to get Phris his freedom as well. But that won't happen now."

"Why not?"

"Marix Ziron's ship was destroyed."

The Hoorinoo sucked in their breath. Several hooted loudly.

"What?" Diego asked.

"Ziron visited our world a few times when he was younger. Usually to survey, but he didn't hesitate to gather more slaves," the female said bitterly.

"Is it permitted to ask your name?"

She nodded. "Hrenssi. I am mated to Hriffen."

Diego inclined his head. "I thank you for your candor. Ziron was the one who captured me as well."

"But you call him by the honorific," she said.

"He chose me as his squire, and I advanced until I

became sub-commander, lower class. At the time of his ship's destruction, Commander Ziron was changing his thinking." Diego remembered his leader with a smile. "Surprisingly, I miss him. Don't ask why, but I do. I came to respect and admire him. I think he respected and trusted me as well."

"Every intelligent creature can progress and change," Hrenssi commented, then changed the subject. "Are you curious why we cover ourselves?"

"I would be lying if I said no. On my world, there is a culture where the females cover up, but I believe it is because of their religion."

"It has nothing to do with our beliefs, only our race's preservation. Our coverings help us avoid capture," Hrenssi began. "Some time ago, the Seressin, as well as the Resh, wanted to have not only males to work but females to propagate the species. It wasn't only to make more slaves, but for our pelts to make decorations for sale on other worlds.

"What?" Diego was confused. "The lavender pelts were used to make things? They killed the Hoorinoo?"

Hrenssi unfastened her covering partway and showed him a pelt of the most exquisite golden orange.

Diego gasped. Not only was the color beautiful, but the female's pelts were longer than the male's. They killed the females for their pelts. He felt sick. "Males are lavender, and females are a gold color."

"Yes," she said, re-fastening her covering.

Hriffen hooted. It didn't sound like laughter. "Perhaps they wonder where we hid our females. When your ship crashed so close to our hidden base, we were worried the Seressin had figured out where our females were. In the past, Seressin and Resh captured females to the point of extinction. The only way we could survive was to hide our girls and women."

"I would be lying if I also didn't ask about your children," Diego said. "I have seen none, even any Hoorinoo the size of

Phris."

"We raise our younglings in a different colony. We established it after a raid that took many of our youth. A few of our males and many of our females take care of the young there."

"That must be hard. Hopefully, you won't have to separate your families for much longer. I think the Seressin are deciding females can be warriors and that they don't have to capture slaves to have enough workers and warriors to man their ships."

"That is good, but it will take a long time before they see us as people and not creatures that supply workers and furs," Hrenssi murmured.

"Maybe, but if I ever get a command of my own, there will be no slaves on board!" Diego responded fervently.

"Are you not in command of this little force?" Hriffen asked.

"Uh." Diego stopped short. "I guess, except I don't have a ship, and we're stranded."

"That makes no difference, Commander Diego." Hriffen stood up. The sky above was dark, void of a moon, but the stars lay like a blanket. "It is time to sleep. We will vacate two of our homes for tonight if that is all right."

"Hriffen, we brought our own tents. Let me show you." Diego called Jeng over. "Pick someone to help you put up a tent."

"We will put up the other one as well, Commander." Before Diego could say a thing, Jeng called Fress, and they pattered off.

"Where do you want two more houses?" Diego asked, chuckling.

"In the space near the tallest house."

Diego conveyed the instructions. Within five minutes, two tents stood rigid near what Diego assumed was Hriffen's dwelling. The reops nickered and then settled down. As everyone headed toward their homes, the colored stones died down but still contained a warm flame in their hearts. Everyone picked one up with heavy woven fabric and carried it to their house.

"You need one in your dwellings," Hrenssi said.

Diego was about to tell her about their supplies that would give light and heat but thought better of it. "Thank you." He thought the light would soothe, even if the heat would be unnecessary. One of the Hoorinoo males carried one into the tent Rrishan showed them. He and Rrishan, and Bress were sharing a tent while the other Turengen slept in the other one.

Rrishan fell asleep immediately. Soon, Bress's breathing slowed, and a slight whistle told him that the Turengen was also sleeping. But as Diego lay there, thoughts whirled around in his head. If no one came to get them, how would they get off-planet? How would they survive? That one Diego didn't worry as much about, but it was the thought of being hunted by the Resh that bothered him. Especially since the toad-like aliens probably knew they were here.

With a sigh, Diego rolled over and gazed at the small blue flame caught in the middle of the mysterious stone. It wasn't exactly a crystal, only semi-opaque. The light in the stone was smaller now but still gave out enough heat to offset the chill of the night air. The blue light was soothing, and as he stared at it, Diego thought of the reop. Compared to a horse on his world, the animal was ugly, but he felt something there — a spirit that almost tied him to it. The more he thought about it, the more he wanted to see what he could do with that reop if, of course, Hriffen let him. That was the last thing he remembered.

CHAPTER THIRTY

An annoying rustling woke Diego. He dreamed of riding the plains on one of his horses. But like most dreams, it was a combination of the here and things before. The blue-violet tint of the waving grass differed from the grasses of the hillside his father's cattle roamed among and ate. Here, the hoofbeats of his and the vaqueros' horses would never pound a pattern. This was not one of his foretelling dreams he had experienced in the past. Diego only assumed those types of dreams ended when Marix Ziron died. With a sigh, Diego opened his eyes and gazed at the top of the tent.

"I didn't mean to wake you," Rrishan said. "I'm sorry."

"Don't worry about it. It's almost sunrise, anyway."

"Can I ask you a question?"

"Of course."

"How long do you think we'll be stranded here?"

Diego sat up. Rrishan sat half-bundled in her sleeping bag. She also looked scared. No, not scared, but uncertain. He shook his head. "I really don't know. I hope not long, but at least if we are, we're with friends."

Silence lingered for several minutes. Diego could hear various animals in the woods chirping, croaking, and peeping.

"Diego, do you think Rreengrol is dead?" Rrishan's whiskers drooped.

"I don't know how any of them could be alive. The *Star*

Devourer blew up. Rreengrol, Ziron, Hreeshan—I don't know."

"I keep hoping...."

"Keep hoping. What happened to Rreengrol and me on Koress was nothing short of miraculous."

She smiled. "Thanks."

"And you'll make every bit as good a warrior as your brother."

"If I get back to Seressin and apprentice to a commander."

"In the meantime, you can apprentice here. I think the Hoorinoos might have some tricks we could all learn."

Rrishan pulled on her jumpsuit and gathered a set of clean clothes. "I'm going to the river and clean up."

"Sounds like a good idea. I'm going to head over to the corral and then probably do the same thing."

"Do you think you can tame one of those things?"

"It's already tame, Rrishan. I'm going to train it."

"Oh." She grinned. "See you in a little while."

Diego didn't doubt his boast. Even his friends had said he was the best horse trainer among the ranchos. Digging through his small pack, he pulled out a nutrition bar that was supposed to be made of some kind of fruit. The taste had a little sweetness, so it would hopefully appeal to a reop. Pulling on his ship suit, Diego slipped on his boots and left the tent. Several of the Hoorinoo females waved at him, and he waved back, continuing to the paddock.

The reops were grazing on a pile of prairie grasses someone had thrown in for their breakfast. Diego stood at the fence and looked for the creature he had interacted with the previous day. Diego made a soft noise and pulled out the nutrition bar. The reop reached its wedge-shaped head over the fence and snorted. Diego broke off a piece and held it out. The deer-horse sniffed it and then grabbed it with leathery lips. Belatedly, Diego hoped nothing in the treat would hurt a reop.

It chewed and then prodded him for more. Before giving it

to him, Diego stroked his jaw. "You will let me ride, won't you?" he whispered, surprising himself. Then the reop reached over and nibbled his hand. He didn't bite. He didn't even pinch. Diego found the animal's nose to be every bit as soft as a horse's from home. The eyes studied him.

Diego examined the ring that hung from his bottom lip. That would have to go. If this animal remained docile enough, he could use a bitless bridle or a hackamore. In fact, from the narrowness of the mouth, that would probably be better for the reop, anyway. The deer-horse snorted and backed away.

"He seems to like you," Hrenssi said quietly, standing beside the human. "What are your plans for this friendship?"

"If it's all right, I'd like to ride him."

"Ride? We have never ridden them. Why would you want to do that?"

"Is there a reason you haven't ridden them, if I may ask?"

She looked up at him; her green shroud parted enough to show a roundish Hoorinoo smile. "First, a reop is quite tall and difficult to mount. A lip ring makes them tractable for leading but wouldn't work for riding."

Diego grinned, found a rope, and worked it into a lasso. He pulled out another piece of the food bar and held it up for the reop to see. It came over and took the treat. Carefully, Diego put the loop around the animal's neck. He snorted but didn't jerk away. When he nudged the human's chest, Diego worked the rope again and put another loop around the reop's nose, well above the nostrils.

The reop shook his head but didn't try to get out of the contrivance. Diego stepped between the slats of the fence and stood beside the animal, giving him another piece of the nutrition bar. Diego led him around the paddock using the rope. By now, he noticed several Hoorinoos and all his crew watching. Diego rubbed along the reop's back and side, the tops of his legs, and down to his hooves. The animal reached around and nibbled on

Diego's rear, which amused him.

He marveled at how quickly this animal adapted to a different type of care. Still, the hard part would be riding. He rubbed along the reop's backbone, finding a natural place to sit behind the withers. Diego continued to rub there, giving the animal the last piece of the bar.

When he stepped back out of the enclosure, the reop whinnied, making a deer-like noise at the end. It stuck its head over the rail, and Diego stroked his nose again. He cut the lead from the make-shift halter. "Let's see how he does with this, and then we can take the lip ring out," Diego said to no one in particular.

"Again, why would you want to ride him?" Hrenssi repeated.

"If I get that far, you'll see. These are muscular animals, and I can imagine they have great stamina. On my world, I rode horses all the time. That was the transportation for our people. Either you rode, or the horses pulled wagons, or you walked." There was another reason, but Diego didn't want to explain his feelings right now.

"That was quite a change for you to be on a spaceship," Hrenssi said.

"Yes, that is why I am so indebted to Phris," Diego said.

CHAPTER THIRTY-ONE

A week later, Diego stood inside the enclosure before dawn and whistled. He didn't need to. The reop he had been working with pranced toward him. He rubbed under the animal's chin and felt the scar from the removal of the ring from its bottom lip. "Let's see if you remember all I taught you." Diego raised his arm, and the reop reared, the cloven hooves pawing the air. A lowered arm, and the animal bowed. Diego made a hand motion, and the reop froze and stayed that way while the young man combed the dusty hide with a rough rag. The reop snorted and pawed the ground in approval when he finished. Diego laughed.

Diego gave Bress charge of day-to-day activities. The Turengen took it upon himself to train the crew. Diego also made a rotating schedule so that one of them always listened to the survey equipment.

When not in training or watching Diego with his reop, Rrishan explored the woods with several of the female Hoorinoos. In addition, she learned the martial arts Diego had been taught during his squire days.

Now, though, Diego wanted to ride his four-legged friend. He created a saddle pad from a woven mat of prairie grasses and part of a ship's blanket sewn together. "Well, my friend, are you ready to try something new?"

The reop whickered and nuzzled his chest. Diego could feel the stump of horn rubbing against his ribs, and he scratched around it. Then he gave his friend a piece of a nutrition bar. Diego attached the rope to the halter and looped it around the reop's neck as reins. Then he laid the pad on the animal's back, tie-straps loose, before leading the creature in a circle. Diego glanced back occasionally to see how the reop adapted to the saddle.

Gazing back at the offending object, the pack animal stomped a cloven hoof and then followed calmly. After a while, Diego stopped and loosely tied the pad's cinch, then repeated the procedure. The reop snorted and stared at his belly this time before following. It gave a hopping skip as though hoping the saddle would fall off.

Diego gave the reop another treat and led him outside the enclosure. Rrishan leaned against the wooden gate, ready to close it after him. All the Turengen looked on except the one on surveillance, as did several of the Hoorinoo. They stayed well back, but their eyes followed his activities with interest. Diego acted surer than he felt. He knew some horses were sedate until they were mounted the first time, then they exploded like kegs of gunpowder.

"My friend, you are going to show me and all these others that you are more than a pack animal. You are strong. You are Fuerte." Diego took a breath. He hesitated to give the reop a name, not knowing if he could ride him. But the name Fuerte felt right. Checking the cinch, he grabbed a handful of ropy mane and swung on.

Fuerte stared back at him in surprise, then snorted. He gave a half-hearted buck, then a stronger one.

Diego clamped his knees against the reop's side. "Use your energy running," Diego cried. "Go. Adelante!" He nudged his heels against the animal's side.

With a grunt of surprise, Fuerte surged forward, almost surprising Diego with the power of his muscular haunches as he leaped forward. When he looked behind him, the reop was far away from the settlement. At first, Diego let him run. He settled forward behind the shoulders and eased his body to Fuerte's gait. The ground they covered was enormous. If he had a reop on Earth, there would be no race he couldn't win. He whooped but stopped when Fuerte shied and almost unseated him.

Another half-mile and Diego pulled back on the reins. Fuerte resisted at first, then eased his pace. The boy began maneuvering him in one direction and then another. Fuerte responded well to the reins despite not having a bit. It exhilarated Diego. The reop slowed to a trot on the way back to the Hoorinoo settlement. This gait jarred him more than the animal's run, but Diego settled into the cadence of that as well. Finally, he pulled him back to a walk, feeling the heat of his mount's body.

As they rode back toward the watchers, Diego leaned forward and gave him a pat on his thick neck. "You are wonderful, my friend."

Fuerte nickered and did a slight prance-skip. He did that all the way to the paddock. Diego slid off and then removed the saddle pad. Using another small blanket, Diego rubbed Fuerte from his nose to his ropy tail. The reop grunted his appreciation. When he cooled down, he gave him some water and more of the survival bar. Twinges in Diego's legs told him he would feel sore later, but it didn't dampen his enthusiasm and joy. He led Fuerte into the paddock and released the lead rope. Fuerte immediately lay down and rolled in the dust. Diego and the others laughed.

That night, Hriffen, Hrenssi, and several other Hoorinoo asked him to teach them how to ride the reops. Rrishan also questioned him about riding. Diego finally promised to tell them more the next day as he crawled into his tent.

He fell asleep immediately.

The next weeks were filled with days of individual and group training sessions. Everyone, it seemed, wanted to ride a reop. Even more intriguing, all the reops were eager to have riders. It seemed as though Fuerte bragged about how much fun it was. Maybe he did, Diego thought.

Each night, he crawled into the tent wearier than any time on the *Star Devourer*. Most of the time, his sleep was dreamless...

Wind whistled through his hair, which Diego tied back with a colorful braided band. His knees clamped against the saddle pad cinched on Fuerte. With an outstretched neck, the deer-like animal raced across the prairie. Never had any of his horses back on the hacienda galloped for as long or as fast as the reops of Nurisna. His beloved Tejas was fast, but not this fast. As much as he hated to admit it, Fuerte superseded Tejas. Only in beauty did Tejas win.

Behind him galloped several other reops, each ridden by a Hoorinoo, Turengen, or Rrishan. Diego felt the animals had waited through the generations to run like this. Over the hills and down, they sped toward the wrecked spaceship. Each trip brought a little more salvage, but this time, something waited; an unknown presence....

Diego jerked awake in the soft glow of one of the crystal stones. Rrishan slept soundly, with soft, mewling sighs punctuating her sleep. Bress, too, breathed deep exhalations of sound sleep. At least Diego had said nothing out loud, or if so, not loud enough to wake his tent-mates.

Had this been a foretelling dream? What lurked out there? Were the Resh coming? The Seressin? Several weeks had passed since his first ride on Fuerte, and the others worked hard to learn to ride the other reops, but they weren't ready to cross the plain to check the wrecked spaceship. So, there had been no salvage efforts. This was the first dream since Marix Ziron's death. In all the time since their crash landing, he felt those kinds of dreams were tied to Commander Ziron. Apparently not.

A glance at his watch told him dawn drew close. Diego knew he wouldn't get back to sleep. Pulling on his jacket, he slipped out of the tent and headed to the paddock. Fuerte nickered, his large head hanging over the top pole, long ears swiveling forward and back. As Diego approached, the reop manipulated the strap holding the gate closed and walked out of the corral. Diego chuckled and shook his head. He fastened the gate behind Fuerte and headed toward the small river to wash up.

Fuerte walked right behind him. When Diego stripped down to his underwear and waded in, the deer/horse took a drink and then splashed Diego as he bathed. The young commander took precautions to put his clothes in a safe place, this time under a large rock. Once before, Fuerte took them, dropping them in the river.

The reop splashed him again. "Madre de Dios! That's cold!" But he laughed even as he splashed the reop back. With a soft noise deep in his throat, Fuerte wandered to a patch of grass and began eating. Diego finished his bath and dressed. Then he gathered the makeshift saddle, the hackamore, a rope, and his side weapon, a small pistol. Fuerte waited for him, just as eager to run as Diego. Quickly, the commander swung into the saddle, and the pair galloped under the thick star canopy of the moonless pre-dawn.

CHAPTER THIRTY-TWO

Diego let Fuerte choose the direction this time. To his surprise, the reop headed directly toward the crashed spaceship. Even while Diego pondered the wisdom of going out there alone, Fuerte opened into a fantastically ground-eating gallop that brought tears to the young man's eyes. The sun came up over the far eastern horizon, almost blinding him, but Diego pulled out his sun goggles from a saddlebag and put them on.

Fuerte continued his phenomenal pace, but Diego didn't slow him. He already knew how much stamina the reops had. Long rides didn't even put them into a lather, as would have happened with horses. The orangish sun was halfway toward its zenith when they reached the ship. The almost two days it took them to walk from the ship to the Hoorinoo settlement, Fuerte accomplished in less than four hours.

Small animals scattered at their approach. When he dismounted, Diego took off the saddle and bridle. Fuerte never tried to run off. The animal seemed content staying with the Hoorinoo and himself. The others were equally happy, especially since the removal of their lip rings.

While Fuerte rolled in the grass and grunted his pleasure, Diego pushed past the damaged hatch, his pistol ready. Only the squeak of a ground creature greeted him. With his hand light, Diego observed that little had been disturbed. The creature, what the Hoorinoo called a flooxiloo, chittered at him and stood, puffed up in its angry posture. Its long body stretched upward until it almost reached Diego's knee. It chattered at him and hissed its displeasure, tiny red eyes boring into his. Diego moved out of its way so it could escape and then checked the cabinets and storage lockers for anything they might have missed.

Some of the metal might be handy for the Hoorinoo. In the small cabins, mess, and other areas not destroyed, Diego found a few more of the survival bars Fuerte loved so much, plus a couple more blankets. He bundled his scavenged items into one of them. After another hour, in which the flooxiloo continued to pop into the ship and gripe at him, Diego picked out what he felt were the most important things to take back. He didn't want to overload Fuerte.

Something on the commander's chair blinked and beeped, startling Diego. He stepped closer, trying to figure out what it might be. Without the one working computer, which they took to the camp, he couldn't tell. Still, Diego realized it had to be part of the detection system and surmised something was nearby or passing overhead. When the blinking faded away, he left the ship. Time to get back and consult with the others.

He took the return trip more slowly, but Fuerte still galloped as though he had rested for days rather than a couple of hours. As he rode, Diego wondered where other reops lived. His observations showed relatively few species, and he also wondered about the wildlife on Nurisna. He hesitated to ask the Hoorinoo. They shared their space, their food, and their reops, but volunteered little information. Diego chose not to pry.

He arrived back at the encampment before dark. Rrishan rode out to meet him, her whiskers laying back against her head. Diego could tell that she was irritated. Before she said anything, he said, "Wait a bit before you tell your commander what he shouldn't have done."

She flicked her tail but only nodded. Then she took the blankets with their salvaged contents while he cared for Fuerte.

As before, the reop rolled on the ground before grazing on the grain-filled grasses gathered that day for the animals. The reops gathered around Fuerte as though he planned on giving them a status report. Diego didn't doubt he would. They nickered, huffed, and snorted together until Fuerte turned his tail and grazed.

"So, what did you find out there?" Rrishan asked.

"We need to have a group meeting so I can tell everyone," Diego replied. Rrishan nodded and followed him to the gathering place.

As before, they laid out the heat stones in a circle around a larger fire. Diego sat with his group. Hriffen and Hrenssi sat nearby.

"You have information and questions," Hrenssi began.

"Yes." Diego took a deep breath. "Last night, I dreamed about Nurisna. I have had such dreams before that guided me." Diego explained what had happened on Koress and how his dreams had guided him and the Seressin. He told of his dream before the Resh destroyed Ziron's ship and how it had changed. "What I dreamed last night was very short and benign except at the end when I felt something waited or watched." Diego shook his head. "I'm not sure if it's something that's already here or will be here, but while I examined the wrecked ship, an indicator came to life and blinked."

At that pronouncement, Bress jerked up in surprise. "Which indicator, Commander?"

"The distance indicator, showing something in orbit, most likely. I would like to believe it's Seressin rescuers, but I can only assume it's the Resh." He turned his attention to the Hoorinoo. "I've had many questions since we crashed on Nurisna, but I haven't asked them. Now, I think our survival may depend on total openness.

"You believe we have hidden information from you?"

Diego was quick to reply. "I think there are things you

have not discussed with us to keep your people safe. Or because of cultural beliefs. I think with the Resh coming, we need more information. We need to work together."

Hriffen spoke to several of the young men. Diego recognized them as three of the most avid riding students. They jumped up, and, working in unison, carried the largest crystal firestone over and set it down in front of Hrenssi. As she leaned forward and gazed into the stone, her shroud dropped off her shoulders. Diego saw that the color of the stone matched the color of her pelt—a bright golden-orange.

Leaning forward, Hrenssi almost touched her forehead to the surface of the stone. Everyone sat perfectly still. Diego wondered at her actions. He was sure the Turengen knew, but he didn't want to disturb anything, even mentally. Insects buzzed outside of the ring of crystals and in the trees beyond their little settlement. Still, Hrenssi lay her head over the stone, unmoving.

Finally, she rose to a sitting position but stooped as though these past moments had aged her. "The only response is one of despair. The group has been discovered."

"The group with your young ones?" Diego ventured.

"Yes." Hrenssi gave a choking cry. "I don't know if they have discovered the eggs."

"Your people lay eggs?" Rrishan asked before she realized she might have been speaking out of turn. "I...."

"It is all right. We should have told you more about our people."

"Please," Diego prompted.

"As we hinted, we keep covered so the enemy doesn't know the differences in our gender. That is also why we keep the younglings apart so that the slavers cannot capture our children. Our main youngling camp is in a valley in the foothills of the mountains. We lay eggs, which are incubated in secret places." She hesitated. "They are deep in the mountains. Not even most of the caretakers know where they are."

"I think we need to take the reops and ride to your valley. Maybe we'll get there in time to save them." At their hesitation, Diego continued. "The reops give us the ability to get there quickly and without being detected. At least we wouldn't be detected as a machine or ship would. If no one has ever ridden reops before, then this will be something the Resh wouldn't be expecting."

No one spoke for what seemed an eternity. The Hoorinoo would have to make this decision.

Hrenssi finally spoke. "You are correct, Diego. We can't just sit here and wait for them to find us. And we must do something for our younglings."

"They may already know we're here," Bress said with a wiggle of his whiskers, "if they had a surveillance satellite or a ship in orbit."

"The best riders will leave in the morning toward the other settlement. Of course, Diego, you will be with the group. Who do you consider the best riders?" Hrenssi asked.

"Rrishan, Jeng, Wissni, Looris…" He named off four more of the Hoorinoo. "Krim will ride with Jeng. Bress, you will be in command of our ground forces. However, if we take all the reops, there will be none to carry your supplies."

Hriffen shook his head. "We will carry what we can on our backs, and the rest of our supplies will stay here buried in the river. Then, we will make haste to the valley settlement. The valley is hard to find, but Wissni and Looris know exactly where it is. They can lead you. The slavers' raids have decimated our people. Now, we need to either fight or lie down and declare our people extinct."

"We'll at least give them a fight!" Diego said.

Hrenssi seemed to shake herself. "I will ride with one of you as well," she declared. "Rrishan, would it bother you for someone to ride behind you?"

"No. It would be an honor."

"Let us prepare and then try to get some sleep."

Diego checked Fuerte's tack and prepared a small pack for the trip. Rrishan and the Turengen did the same.

"If it is Resh, they will be surprised," Bress declared with a toothy grin.

"Or we will," Diego muttered.

"Commander," Hrenssi called.

"Yes?"

"I must take the crystal. It allows for communication. I realize it's heavy, but would your reop be willing to take it along with you?"

"Of course. Did the reops carry them when you moved?"

"They pulled the cart that held them all."

"Regardless, I would be happy to take it.

CHAPTER THIRTY-THREE

Diego and his tent-mates were awake before the sun rose. Fuerte nickered from the paddock as the young man exited the tent with his pack. The other reops milled behind.

Diego saddled and bridled Fuerte, who pawed at the ground with his hoof. There were plenty of the survival bars and a container of water in his saddlebag, Diego noted. Extra weapons, those not taking up much room, and a blanket finished out his supplies. The others were breaking camp. Diego scratched his friend's forehead.

The rest of the riders saddled the other reops. Diego modified a blanket to use as a sling for the crystal stone. He tied another blanket-sling on the other side and equalized the weight with another of the crystals—one that Hriffen had picked out. Diego used extra pieces of the blanket to pad the slings.

"Commander," Bress began. "Do you have any orders?"

Diego shook his head. "Bress, make sure you bring all the weapons you can and teach the Hoorinoo their use on the way to the rendezvous."

"It will be accomplished as ordered," Bress replied formally.

Diego mounted. The others followed his lead. The reops seemed to pick up the emotions of their riders, prancing and snorting. "We will prevail." Diego saluted the warriors he was leaving behind.

One of the Hoorinoo riders led the troop out onto the prairie and headed north toward a dark horizon that seemed even more sinister because of what might be there—or what might not. Their route ran almost parallel to the river, which flowed south. Occasionally, it widened, while other times, it transformed into a swift-flowing stream. A variety of trees grew along the riverbanks.

The reops didn't run all out as Fuerte did before, but it was still a ground-eating gallop. Occasionally, they would slow to a butt-breaking trot. Even the Hoorinoo riders felt the jarring gait through their thick pelts. They didn't resort to a trot very often.

By midday, the large forest fell far behind them. Now, they were traveling through the prairie grass. Diego worried about their visibility, but nothing flew overhead, and they kept close to any small stands of trees. A little after midday, they halted under a tree and ate their trail rations.

"How far is this other settlement, Hrenssi?" Diego asked.

"We have only walked it before, so I cannot accurately tell you how long it will take us, but I am guessing we have already ridden the equivalent of two day-cycles."

Diego nodded. "And how many day-cycles does it take for your people to walk the distance?"

"Almost ten."

"Then, if all goes well, it should take us two, maybe three, days of steady riding to get there."

"Yes, Commander, but the hills will rise, and the valleys deepen, slowing us up."

"And we will need to approach carefully, too."

"Yes, we will. The river will also deepen, but there will be stands of trees," Hrenssi informed him.

"Good." Diego checked on Fuerte and found him breathing normally and grazing lightly. He led his deer-like friend to the river to get a drink. They continued their journey until the sun set on the tops of the western hills.

Looris hooted, calling a halt at a place that appeared to have been inhabited at one time. Diego felt nervous staying someplace an enemy might know. "Is it wise to spend the night in a place the Resh might have knowledge of?" he asked the Hoorinoo.

With a small hoot, Looris looked to Hrenssi for advice.

"Yes, you are right, Commander," she replied with a sigh.

Diego knew the Hoorinoo wise woman felt the effects of the long ride but had not complained at all. "Why not go a little further and see if there is anything more protected and less used?"

"I will walk a little while," Hrenssi said, sliding off Rrishan's reop. She landed with a grunt and then walked behind the troop. Jeng slid off from behind Krim and walked with the Hoorinoo.

Diego and Looris rode together up front, looking for a place where they would be secure. At a bend in the river, they found a small clearing surrounded by tall trees and thick brush. They made their camp there. When Diego took off Fuerte's saddle pad and bridle, the reop trotted to the river, where he waded in. The other reops followed his lead, and soon, they were grunting and snorting in the water. Amazingly, they must have understood this special mission because they played and grazed silently.

Rrishan approached, watching their mounts. "Were your horses like this?"

"Yes, a little, but I don't think they were as intelligent and eager to do what we wanted. While I miss my horses, I am enjoying the reops. They have much more stamina and strength than a horse."

"I wish I could take Rashti home with me."

Diego felt a pang of sadness. If they were ever rescued, he knew he would have to leave Fuerte. He pushed that aside. "What does Rashti mean?" Diego knew the Grrlock language, but he never heard this word before.

"Rashti was a mythological creature that tried to fly to the sun. It had large wings and claws to rip open the clouds and let the rain fall to the parched ground. The sun hoarded it from the dying Grrlocks when he got angry with them. Rashti died before reaching the sun, and Sun felt sorry for doing such a thing. It never withheld the rain that long again."

To Diego, it sounded a little like some myths of his childhood. "That's a great name for your reop."

"What about Fuerte?"

"It means strong in Spanish."

Rrishan chuckled. "That's an excellent name, too."

Two Turengen offered to take turns guarding the camp since they were telepathic. Diego and Rrishan joined the rotation.

Before they pulled out their evening rations, Hrenssi laid her head on the crystal and tried to contact the other Hoorinoo. She succeeded with Hrissen but not with the group ahead of them. For almost an hour, she kneeled with her head against the crystal, then she sighed and rose to her feet. With a hoot, she announced. "I do not know the condition of the settlement ahead. Hriffen and the others are well, but I feel danger ahead of us."

"Krim and Jeng will help us avoid going into a trap," Rrishan said.

"Yes, I know. I think it would be wise to get to sleep as soon as possible," the Hoorinoo said.

Even with the reops' stamina, a full day of riding sapped a rider's energy. "I agree," Diego said. Still, he took the first guard rotation at the top of the tallest hill as the reops grazed below. Occasionally, they nickered to one another, but otherwise, the camp was quiet. Too quiet, Diego thought. There should be more night noises. He jumped when Fuerte nuzzled him behind the ear. The reops' ability to move silently was almost spooky, but he rubbed under his friend's jaw.

Then Fuerte stiffened, huffing the night air.

"What is it?" Diego whispered, slowly getting to his feet. He could sense it. Something out there watched them.

CHAPTER THIRTY-FOUR

Fuerte grunted and turned toward several large shapes appearing out of the dark. Diego pulled on his night lenses and saw what they were—reops. Their lip rings told him they were domesticated. The dragging ropes suggested they had escaped from another camp.

Fuerte rubbed against the nearest one, nickering. Diego reached out for its rope, and the reop shied away. Fuerte continued communicating with them. Their own reops joined the new group, and a soft conversation occurred between them. Diego heard footsteps behind him and laid his hand on his pistol before he realized it was Hrenssi.

"These are from the other camp." She reached out and took the lead rope of the closest reop.

"The best I can tell, there are eight of them," Diego told her.

"There are usually about ten with each settlement. I think there were a few more with this group."

"I know we're close, but how close?"

"Several valleys," Hrenssi said.

"Stay here. I'm going to reconnoiter. I don't see a glow, so I don't think the Resh have set up a camp there. Of course, I could be mistaken."

"I am going with you. I have to—in case they have harmed our people."

Diego nodded. He woke Jeng and Krim. "Jeng, I want you to come with Hrenssi and me. We need you to listen to any mental chatter. Krim, you'll have to take my guard duty. Hopefully, we'll be back before dawn."

Jeng nodded and melted into the darkness. Soon, she came back with her reop, bridled but unsaddled, as well as Rrishan's reop for Hrenssi to ride. "Apparently, the Resh are not worried about wandering reops, so they should not mind a group of three 'aimless' reops in the area—if they are camped nearby."

"A good point." Diego mounted. One of the camp reops followed. It allowed Diego to unhook the lip ring.

They rode without speaking, Jeng in the lead, the loose reop following behind. As before, it amazed Diego how sure-footed they were in the dark.

This three-valley trip felt like an eternity. His nerves jangled, and he finally practiced one of his relaxation exercises.

The group rode through a depression between two hills and then up a rise. Jeng motioned for them to lie as flat as they could on their reops' backs. They crossed over and started down a rock-strewn hill. Now Diego detected a slight glow beyond the next hill. When they paused at a small stream in the valley beyond, Jeng gave a signal to stop. The Turengen slid off his mount, and Diego followed his example. Hrenssi joined them.

"What are you picking up?" Diego whispered.

"Resh. They invaded the camp where most of the women are living."

Hrenssi moaned. "Are my people still there?"

"I believe they all are, but I don't know how many were there to begin with."

Hrenssi was quick to answer. "There were twenty-two females and twelve guards."

Jeng shook her head. "I can't tell for sure, but the mind chatter seems less than thirty-four individuals."

"Where is their main camp?" Diego asked.

Jeng paused, her eyes closed. Then she pointed to the east. "I think they are sending another shuttle to pick up the group we left behind."

"Do they know about the eggs?" Hrenssi asked.

"If they do, I am not hearing anything in their minds about it. Perhaps they don't want to deal with embryonic beings."

"Can we get to the main camp before sunrise? If they take our people off-planet, we will lose them," Hrenssi whispered.

"No," Diego replied. "We save these first and then head to the main camp. Jeng, can you warn the others to break camp?"

The Turengen nodded, and the trio crept back to the reops. The others were already approaching, apparently warned by Jeng. The new reops followed behind them.

"We are going to save the captive Hoorinoos," Diego explained, trying to figure out a safe battle plan. He remembered his experience with cattle and horse herds. "I have several of the concussion bombs that can cause havoc, but I think a stampede would be most appropriate in this case. It would seem more natural."

"Stampede?" Hrenssi asked.

"It is an uncontrolled run of a group of animals. They can really create havoc in a small area. If the unridden reops charge into the Resh camp, then we follow and free the Hoorinoo before the Resh realize what happened. Animals this size can do some damage."

"Wouldn't the Resh have some kind of protective force shield for their camp?" Rrishan asked.

"We'll have to find that out by sending in the reops. If the Resh have one, the first reop will be shocked, and they will turn back," Diego said.

"I found nothing to indicate such a thing in this camp," Jeng added. "That doesn't mean there isn't, but they might be too sure of their superiority."

"Or too complacent. There really don't seem to be any

large animals on the plains and in the hills besides the reops," Diego added. "Still, we don't have time to debate. Let's go do what we can."

This time, Jeng and Diego led the group along a valley path through the darkness. By his best reckoning, the night was half gone. The group traveled single file. The reops maintained a fast trot in the darkness, never stumbling or kicking up rocks.

Finally, Jeng stopped in an area where the path widened. "I'll get the other reops," he whispered and rode back down the trail toward the free animals still following. Jeng sent Diego a mental picture of a rush of animals going over the hill and down a slope into a flat area. Then he saw a picture of a vehicle, multiple metal legs holding up the dark gray body like a bloated spider.

Diego studied the blurry picture for anything to help them. Looris urged the loose reops up the trail toward the hill. Diego followed, motioning to the Hoorinoo the best way to stampede the animals. Looris signaled his agreement. Eight animals trotted up the hill. As the last reop passed by, Diego slapped it on the rump. It hooted and lurched forward. The others sped up to avoid being trampled.

Diego urged Fuerte against the last reop's rump. To his surprise, Fuerte bit the other one just above its tail. The small herd moved faster. Their cloven feet thundered a tattoo on the hard ground. They picked up speed, approaching the crest of the hill. Diego sent a message to the Turengen to watch for a force shield. The reops crested the rise and rushed down the other side.

There was a croaking cry as they galloped down to the valley where the shuttle sat. Fuerte gave a shrill, ear-piercing scream, and several other reops joined him. A Resh aimed his rifle, but someone in the attack group fired a laser shot. There was a gurgling scream. Then, the reops rushed through the camp, knocking down Resh and trampling their equipment. Diego and the rest used their stun pistols to neutralize the Resh guards.

Before Fuerte stopped, Diego leaped off and ran to the

entrance of the Resh ship. A guard fired from the hatch. A reop screamed, then a Hoorinoo. Diego rolled behind a fallen Resh soldier, firing as he hit the ground. He pulled out another weapon and changed the setting. A wide stun spray might have a better chance of disorienting the Resh guard. He fired, and a gurgling croak told him he had scored. The Resh tumbled out the doorway and lay still on the ground.

"We'll take care of any others inside," Diego ordered, motioning to Rrishan, Krim, and Jeng. "You three, follow. Now!" Diego hissed. They rushed inside the shuttle. Hrenssi followed them.

CHAPTER THIRTY-FIVE

"Keep your heads down!" Diego ordered.

Rrishan grinned and moved behind a control panel. They shot down a corridor. Diego wanted to neutralize the Resh before they could harm their prisoners. He motioned for Rrishan and Krim to continue firing while he and Jeng rushed forward.

With her telepathic ability, the Turengen determined the remaining enemy positions. It didn't take long for them to clear the corridor.

Diego nudged one of the fallen enemy with his toe. "We need to restrain or confine them somewhere where they won't bother us."

"Perhaps in the confinement units, where they have the Hoorinoo?" Rrishan suggested.

Diego nodded. "That's a great idea, at least for the moment."

"We need to get the prisoners out first," Jeng said.

Diego nodded. "Krim, let the others know we have control of the ship. Hrenssi, I don't think we need more than one or two."

As Krim pattered off, Jeng said, "You feel something is not right?"

Diego nodded. "I think we need to get all non-essential personnel out and away before those other Resh and their second shuttle come to investigate. I don't think we'll be able to use this craft."

"Like the Koressian vehicles?"

"Maybe, or some other nasty surprise." Diego wished he knew why he felt suspicious. It seemed like a clean operation.

The Hoorinoo joined them, and together, they discovered the units where the women and youngsters were held. The younger Hoorinoo had various colors of fur. Their hoods and robes were missing, making it appear like a rainbow had settled in the prison units. "The Resh know," Hrenssi muttered. "They know about our females."

"Don't worry about that. Get them out of here. Now!" Diego's weird feelings had intensified, and the Turengen's silence and frantic pace to get everyone out just added to his anxiety. "Hrenssi, is there anywhere you might hide them from the Resh scouts and ships?"

"There are some low mountains and hills to the north." Hrenssi began.

"Take them there. We'll find you later."

Hrenssi's round blue eyes looked deep into his eyes. "What are you afraid of?"

"A trick. I think the Resh have something else planned. I don't know. Take all the reops except Fuerte and Krim's. Krim, you stay with our reops."

Looris escorted a large group of Hoorinoo down the corridor. They hooted their relief, hurrying to get away from a future with the Resh. Hrenssi led another group.

Diego counted over twenty Hoorinoo. "Is that everyone?"

"Wissni is checking with your Grrlock warrior," Hrenssi called out as they passed out of sight.

"Jeng, stay by the hatch. I don't want us caught inside."

"Why don't we try to fly it out?" the Turengen asked.

Diego wondered at his previous misgivings. *Why don't we?* Then he had an idea. "Are there any Resh who are coming back to consciousness?"

"I am feeling one nearby. It's the guard near the hatch."

"Try to see if you can get anything out of his mind. A way to pilot this shuttle."

Jeng nodded. "Yes, Commander." She scampered down the corridor.

Wissni and Rrishan ran toward him with a dozen more Hoorinoo youth. Some had lavender pelts, some reddish-gold, and some golden. "These are the last prisoners."

"Good. Wissni, you take them to Hrenssi. Everyone is heading to the mountains to find a hiding place. You might be giving quick riding lessons."

Wissni hooted with laughter. "Yes, much quicker than running through the grass." They pattered down the corridor to the outer hatch.

Rrishan waited with Diego, holding her weapon ready. "Let's get out of here."

Jeng's thoughts came into Diego's mind. *Commander! Ship is going to explode! They set the ship to explode as we attacked.*

Diego motioned to the others, and they sprinted down the corridor.

Jeng caught up with them. "The Resh thought they would defeat us, and then they would cancel the destruction. I felt his triumph that the explosion would still kill us."

"Faster! We have little time!"

The three of them ran as fast as they could, their feet echoing in the empty corridors. Diego figured they reached the hatch in record time. "Jeng, ride with me. Rrishan with Krim. Warn the others."

Soon, they were thundering not too far behind the large group of Hoorinoos. Diego also called a warning, and the company urged more speed from their animals. The untrained reops were running without riders, but the others had at least four or five Hoorinoos on their backs. Diego saw the reops struggling beyond their capacity. Diego took two smaller Hoorinoos from overwhelmed mounts, and Rrishan did the same.

They rushed over a small hill and down an incline into a valley with a few trees and a stream.

Diego would have liked getting to the next valley, but they had been fortunate to have made it as far as they did. "As many as possible, take cover," Diego yelled. The Hoorinoos slid off the reops and hunkered down in the grass, the older ones huddling over the younger ones. "Hur...."

A monstrous explosion shook the ground. Sure-footed Fuerte stumbled, and Diego half-slid, half-fell off. Shortly after that, a shock wave threw them both off their feet. The last thing he remembered was rolling away from his mount to avoid getting squashed.

***

Diego felt something cool against his face. It laid on him, and he reached up to push it away—a cloth, damp and cool in the wind blowing down from the tops of the hills.

Hrenssi hooted. "Commander. You need to wake up."

"I'm awake," he mumbled. Diego opened his eyes to glaring sunlight. Lowering his lids and sitting up, he noticed ash and small chunks of debris peppered the ground. Then he remembered the Resh ship. "Anyone hurt?"

"Like you, most were knocked to the ground, but we are very thankful there are no serious injuries," Hrenssi replied.

"The Resh most likely will return to this area when they realize what happened to their ship." With Jeng's help, he stood up. Rrishan lay curled up on the ground, unconscious. "Is she alright?"

Jeng nodded. "Yes. She will awaken shortly."

"How are the reops?"

"Some ran from the explosion; a few have returned," Hrenssi told him. "They have cuts and minor injuries from flying debris."

"Those who are unconscious or have injuries will ride the reops available. Let me know if you can't hang on to the unconscious," Diego ordered. "Those well enough, walk. We need to get under cover, either in the hills or in the woods, before the other Resh come."

The disheveled group helped their companions. Then, they plodded a steady course toward the distant hills, listening for the high-pitched whine of a Resh spacecraft.

By late afternoon, Looris found a wooded area where they could all rest. Not long after that, Diego's ears picked up the sound of a spacecraft. "Hurry! They're coming." He ran to the relative safety and shade of the trees. The whine passed overhead and then diminished. Diego slumped down against the thick trunk of a tree, listening. Fuerte nudged his foot and grunted. Finally, there were no more sounds from the sky other than a few birds.

"Do you think it's gone?" Rrishan asked. She sported a bruise in front of one ear and a lump on the back of her head.

Diego shook his head. "No. Sounds more like they landed somewhere not too far away. We'll need to check it out, but not before dark."

CHAPTER THIRTY-SIX

"We need to find a safer place for all our people," Hrenssi said, sitting close by.

"Go as deep into the wilderness as you can and hide. Make it hard for the Resh to find any of your people."

"What are you going to do?"

"What I wanted to do with the ship that exploded—capture the investigating vessel."

"We wish you all the good fortune available," Hrenssi said. She gathered the other Hoorinoo and several of the reops. Within a short while, they left. The caravan soon disappeared.

"I want to find out if they captured the others," Diego added, remembering how vulnerable Bress and the others would be walking on the prairie.

Jeng chittered. "Krim and I can sneak close and listen."

"They will be on their guard."

"I know," Jeng agreed.

"Wait until dark. That's only a few hours away."

Jeng sighed and sat down. She curled up and fell asleep. Several other Turengen joined her.

Diego rose to his feet and shuffled over to Fuerte. The reop nuzzled his chest while Diego checked Fuerte for cuts and abrasions. He found nothing serious, but he knew his friend was worn out. They all needed a good night's sleep. He slid back down against another tree trunk.

Rrishan handed him a meal bar and sat down next to him. "Are you all right?"

"Just tired. And you?"

"I'm fine. A little headache."

"A good night's sleep would help us all."

Rrishan snorted. "Fat chance of getting one of those anytime soon."

Diego chuckled. He could count on one hand the number of full nights of sleep he'd received in the past year. "Actually, it was tanning season on my home world when Ziron captured me. Few complete nights then, either."

"What's tanning season?" Rrishan chewed on her meal bar.

"It's when the cows are gathered in from the hills, and many of them butchered for meat and hides. The hides are prepared, or tanned, to make leather for various things like clothing and saddles."

"Oh. You butchered your own animals? Are those cows like the reops?"

"I helped, and, yes, they are a little like them, but I wouldn't dream of riding on a steer or a cow." Diego yawned and took a bite of his tasteless bar. "Tiring of these. Wouldn't mind butchering a fat steer." He explained that term, too.

"I'm glad we get our food already processed. Not sure I'd enjoy eating something I had just killed."

Diego smiled. He had eaten the fruits of other people's labors for long enough to forget the details of a fiesta with his family.

"Why don't you rest further back into the trees, and I'll watch for Jeng and Krim after they go out," Rrishan suggested.

Diego wanted to disagree, but he couldn't. "If I sleep too long, wake me up when they return." With a sigh, he rose and walked among the trees. He pulled out his blanket and curled up on the softest patch of ground he could find. Diego had no memory of even laying his head down.

He awoke to pitch darkness. He only saw two sets of bright eyes gazing at him in the dark. "I hope you haven't been sitting there long." Diego sat up. He shivered and pulled the blanket tighter, then looked around for Rrishan.

"She is guarding the camp," Jeng answered his thought.

Krim spoke. "We have not been sitting here long."

Diego nodded and stretched out some kinks. "So, what did you find out?"

"They landed about halfway between the destroyed ship and here. It is a scout craft with ten Resh crewmembers, five of them soldiers. They are setting up a camp. Several of the Resh took some kind of land vehicle and headed toward their destroyed ship. They stay in their ship when they are not doing specific outside tasks. And they do not have any of our people from the other camp. Nor do they have any Hoorinoo."

"That's good news." He let his mind digest all the information. "They are being more careful."

"Yes, Commander," Jeng answered. "They appear to be paying attention to anything coming close to their camp, including animals. We coaxed one of the loose reops into meandering toward the camp, and a mild force shield shocked her before she could get too close."

"That makes it hard to take the ship."

"We will watch. Let them get complacent," Krim suggested.

"That may be the only thing we can do right now. You two get something to eat and then rest." Diego could be patient, but waiting was to the Resh's advantage. They were closer to their home world and had more resources.

"We found something to eat on the way to the Resh ship. But we will rest."

As the Turengen settled down, curled up next to each other, Diego slipped out of camp to where he presumed Rrishan stood guard. A pistol in his side told him he had found her. Diego dropped the blanket and held out his hands. "You are good at this," he said with a smile.

"Oh, Commander. Sorry."

"Don't be. You are guarding our camp; you did right. I can take over; you've been here quite a while."

"Not tired," she said, stifling a yawn.

"Liar." Diego smiled. "How long have you been out here? Half the night?"

"Since Jeng and Krim went scouting."

"You know that part of being a squire is following a superior's commands, right?"

"Of course, but we are shorthanded."

"As a warrior in the Seressin forces, rank of sub-commander third class, I hereby enlist Rrishan, a capable warrior from the planet Grrlock, as a squire and warrior-in-training. Do you, Rrishan, accept assignment as squire to Sub-Commander Bress and Sub-Commander Diego Perez?"

She paused and then gave him a soft 'yes.'

"Good, you are now a member of the Seressin forces — in training." He paused. "Go get some sleep." When she hesitated, he added, "That's an order."

There was a soft hiss, and then she laughed. It reminded Diego of Rreengrol. "All right, Commander." She padded off.

A few moments later, Diego heard a soft footfall and then a nicker almost in his ear. He reached up and scratched under Fuerte's chin. The reop stood behind him, perfectly still, until dawn. As the reddish light glowed beyond the eastern horizon, Diego saddled Fuerte and rode him toward the ship. By the time he reached the hill overlooking the Resh encampment, it had grown light enough to reconnoiter. He left Fuerte in a small stand of trees and bushes, and crouching low, Diego continued down the hill. He watched for any guards, but seeing none, he could only believe they were relying on their machines.

Halfway down the hill, hidden by brush, Diego lay on his

stomach and watched for any activity. A lone Resh in full battle armor march-hopped around the ship. He occasionally checked a device strapped to his skinny arm. Diego reconnoitered until more Resh came out of the ship. The guard pulled off the device and handed it to one of the others, talking in his croaking speech and gazing up the hill toward Diego's hiding place.

He waited for a few more minutes before slipping away. Mounting Fuerte, he trotted back toward camp. Jeng met him.

"They may know we're here. At least they acted like they knew I was watching them," Diego told her. "They did nothing about it, but it makes me very uncomfortable."

Jeng looked thoughtful. "I picked up nothing from their minds that they were aware of you near their camp. Maybe we should try to steal the ship."

Diego shook his head. "No, not now. There are too many of them. Too risky."

"What's too risky?" Rrishan asked, yawning and stretching. Diego told her what he had seen.

"You think the Resh knew you were there, but Jeng couldn't pick up on it?" she asked. Then she turned toward Jeng. "Did it seem like their thoughts were protected?"

Jeng shook her head. "No, I felt thoughts, although they are harder to pick up than from you or the commander."

Diego paced the small campground, trying to think. Fuerte nudged his hand, clenching the uneaten bar. Diego broke it in half and gave part of it to his friend. Then, a wild thought stopped him in his tracks.

"No, we cannot take the ship right now, but why not take the land vehicle?"

The others just stared at him for a moment, and then the Turengen began chittering.

Rrishan grinned. "When Commander?"

"Now! Let's break camp, figure out the best route, and see how fast the reops can go! Hide some of the less necessary things, like sleeping bags and other camp gear. We need to ride light so we can travel fast."

By the time the sun was a little above the horizon, they were ready. Diego figured out the best route to the wrecked ship. They each had a reop, and Diego was eager for more of the mile eating gallop Fuerte had shown him before. The reops didn't disappoint them. Fuerte set the pace, his cloven hooves beating a soft rhythm against the dry ground. Diego finally saw some of the hidden wildlife of the area. Snakes with multiple skinny legs scurried out of their path along with hissing purple lizards and small mammals that dived into mounds at the base of the trees.

As before, Diego reveled in the wind blowing against his face. He felt at home on the back of a reop.

The sun was directly overhead when Diego ordered a pause. "We're getting closer, and they could have something out to detect us."

Jeng pulled out their detection device. She worked the controls of the fist-sized device. "Only a little way farther. So far, I am not seeing evidence of the Resh detecting us, but we cannot feel their thoughts yet, either."

They reached the area of the destroyed ship about mid-afternoon. A brisk wind brought the stench of burned metal. It also brought the sound of the Resh talking. He couldn't hear noises indicating the land machine was going anywhere soon. Good.

"This way," Diego said, pointing to a stream with a grassy path beside it.

They rode farther, Jeng constantly checking her device. "We are close. Am hearing a few thoughts. I do not believe there are detection devices."

Diego stopped and dismounted. Everyone else did the same. He left Fuerte's reins loose, and then he crept up the hill toward the wrecked ship, pistol drawn. The others followed. Single file, the group worked their way through the brush and around a hill to spy on the Resh. One warrior hopped in sight, studying the debris on the ground. He waddled to a large piece and bent low to pick it up.

"Where are the others?" Rrishan whispered. "We heard them."

The Resh stood and looked around. Was their hearing that good?

One is inside. I hear another one's thoughts, but not sure where he is.

Diego heard a noise behind them and then Fuerte's coughing call. He motioned for the others to take care of the two Resh warriors in front of them while he backtracked to the reops. He slipped through the brush, stopping and listening every few minutes. There was the snap of a twig, the crunch of a broken leaf, and Diego knew where the missing Resh had disappeared.

Fuerte grunted again, and Diego slipped toward him. He peered past a bush and saw a Resh examining the reops, his pistol held in his three-fingered hand. Diego drew and fired before the Resh could move another step. The scout collapsed with a gurgling croak. Fuerte nickered, and the other reops pulled on their bridles.

Diego rushed to grab them before they could run away, making soothing sounds. The smallest one, Krim's reop, jerked out of his hand, jumped over the tiny stream, and ran out of sight. Diego held the remaining two tighter. "Stay here," he whispered to Fuerte, also making a hand sign. The reop nickered.

Diego checked the unconscious Resh, stripping him of any weapons he could find. Next, he took the creature's belt and tied his hands tightly together. Exerting extra effort, Diego dragged the scout into the brush. He trotted back to where he had left the Turengen and Rrishan. They were already in the Resh camp. One guard lay on the ground. Then Diego heard a croaking scream from inside the exploration vessel.

He dashed into the ship and skidded to a stop. Krim

chittered at him. "Enemy neutralized."

"Where's Rrishan?"

"Commander, who do you think neutralized the last Resh?"

Rrishan walked toward him with a feral grin. "The enemy vessel is captured, Commander. I'm sorry I didn't take the last Resh alive. He was intent on killing me."

"Understandable. Well done. Gather all weapons and get him out of here. We're going to rendezvous with our comrades."

"What about the reops?" Rrishan asked.

"I will take them with me as I ride to the Resh ship. Can you drive this to the Resh encampment?"

With a chitter, Jeng trotted to the controls. After several minutes of study and tinkering, the land explorer started up with a muttering growl that changed to a muted purr. Jeng grinned.

Diego nodded. "I will take the reops back toward the Resh encampment while you head back with the land explorer. I can provide a diversion to divide the Resh even more. Make it easier for you to drive into the camp and take the ship."

"Perhaps the land explorer can develop problems outside of the camp," Jeng suggested.

"Excellent suggestion." Diego gazed around at his small troop of warriors.

"It's almost night," Krim observed. "That might help, too."

"Let's head out. We will stop a mile outside their camp and reconnoiter again. Take care of the other Resh. He will eventually get loose, but without a communicator, he won't interfere with our plans."

"We will prevail," Rrishan intoned.

"We certainly will," Diego responded. After finding a rope among the Resh supplies, Diego strode back to the reops. The fourth one had returned and grazed with the others. Diego tied the animals in a long line with his rope. After mounting, he pulled on the lead line, and the other three animals followed.

"I hope you have had a long enough rest," Diego told the creatures. "Let's see if you run as fast going back as you did coming." The sun was already approaching the western horizon.

The reops broke into a gallop. Diego leaned forward, letting the short mane tickle his nose. For long runs, Diego had found it more relaxing laying along Fuerte's thick neck and withers. It was also easier on his backside as well, although he had become quite used to riding a reop in either position.

As the sun disappeared behind the hills, Diego heard a soft whining that grew in volume. It came from ahead and was approaching extremely fast.

CHAPTER THIRTY-SEVEN

As the whining sound increased, Diego realized there was no place to hide four reops in the grasslands, so he waited, weapon drawn. The rope tied around his waist would be a detriment in a fight, so he untied it. Again, he lay prone against his reop's neck, this time to make himself a smaller target.

We are not the enemy, Commander. It was a faint thought, but Diego recognized Jeng and sighed in relief. He gathered the rope and waited. Soon, he heard the grinding of metal parts, the whine of an engine, and the bite of the wheels churning over the hard earth. The land crawler was approaching. Fuerte's cloven hoof dug at the soil, and the other reops pranced but didn't try escaping. The vehicle pulled to within twenty feet of where he waited and stopped. The engine powered down, and one of his three comrades opened the hatch.

"Can you tell if the Resh know we're here?" Diego asked when the Turengen climbed out.

"Nothing on the communicator and we are too far away to feel any Resh thoughts," Jeng said. "Not that it was easy before. Harder to follow a Resh's thoughts than yours."

Diego chose not to say anything about that. "You made good time."

"It took a while to figure out how to run the machine, and the controls are a little different, but Squire Rrishan is an excellent driver. She made up for lost time."

"You all did a great job."

Jeng and Krim waited for instructions while Diego thought furiously. The stampede idea wouldn't work again. Or would it? They'd have to see how this all played out. Then, he remembered Jeng's idea. "Would a distraction draw some of them away? Your idea, Jeng? We'd have a better chance of taking their ship if we didn't have to fight so many."

"I didn't see explosive devices on the land explorer, or we could use those. Of course, we didn't search." Jeng said.

"Regardless, I want to see our latest offensive weapon," he said with a grin. "Do you mind standing guard, Krim?" Dusk quickly gave way to full darkness.

"Will do that, Commander."

Diego ducked through the hatchway. Resh were squatty like toads, and though they were large, they weren't tall. Rrishan sat in the pilot's chair, watching a monitor. "Good driving," Diego told her.

"I learned to drive similar vehicles at home. Our larger transports are like these, too, and my sire has taken me out in his."

"Another ready-made skill." He opened the cabinets and dug through the contents. Some appeared to be food preserved in clear plastic, but he ignored those. They were squishy and bile green. There were a few creature comforts, like blankets and clothes. Once again, he ignored them.

"Here, Commander," Jeng called out. He was in the back of the vehicle.

Diego joined him and saw the treasure trove of weapons in a large cabinet. There were a half-dozen pistols, the same number of rifles, and several smaller boxes with what appeared to be bombs of various sizes. "I wonder if they stored most of their weapons here."

"Or maybe they have even more on their ship," Jeng suggested, pulling out a box.

"Could that be why the other ship went up with such a tremendous explosion?" Diego motioned his crew over for a strategy meeting. "I don't have a lot of ideas left, but I think a diversion to get them to lower their defensive shield is the only way to do this. If you just tried to go in, you don't have the codes or passwords to make them think their comrades are returning. I don't want to take a chance of them having the firepower to destroy the land explorer."

Diego paused, still thinking about the military tactics of his own country. He knew it was far beneath what these star travelers had, but there might be some merit to primitive tactics. "Let's figure out how to detonate these bombs. Then I'll carry a pouch of them, riding Fuerte, and explode them outside of the perimeter of their defense. I can make a circle, setting off the devices in different places."

"Do you think the defensive device alone will explode them?" Rrishan asked.

"I think we should find out." He started out of the vehicle.

"Commander?" Jeng asked.

"Yes?"

"I think either myself or Krim should accompany you. It would be more effective if two bombs went off simultaneously."

Diego deliberated, rubbing his chin. "You're right. There should be two of us. Krim will ride with me."

"Perhaps there should also be a short period of rest and refreshment before heading out on this foray," Rrishan suggested.

Diego was eager to begin this sortie, but he agreed. It had been a long, hard day. There was a benefit to waiting until after dark to make this attack. By then, the Resh might be more complacent. "It's very good to have superior warrior companions."

While they ate more of the sustenance bars, which Diego noted were almost gone, they examined the bombs, trying to figure out how they detonated without testing one. The Turengen curled up and dozed off. Diego tried, but was unable. A slight purring nearby told him Rrishan had fallen asleep. A soft buzzing jerked Diego awake — his watch. Apparently, he had dozed off as well. Everyone sat up, stretching.

"Let's see what we can do." Diego almost said, 'We will prevail!' But it seemed redundant. They were warriors. They had to prevail. He and Krim mounted, each with a pouch of the Resh bombs. They trotted away from the vehicle.

At a safe enough distance from the Resh spaceship, Diego pulled out a bomb and urged Fuerte into a slow gallop. He lobbed the device toward the ship. It bounced off the shield, hit the ground, and sat there. "Too far out," he muttered.

They tightened their circle. The hairs rose on the back of his neck, and he presumed it was the effect of the defensive shield. He pulled out another bomb, pushed a button on the bottom of the weapon, and threw it. Before it was halfway to the ground, it exploded. Krim tossed his, and it also exploded.

As fast as he could, Diego pulled out bombs and tossed them. Behind him, Krim did the same. They rode all the way around once and then pulled away.

Diego only had a few more of the devices. "Do you feel anything from the Resh, Krim?"

"Yes, and I hear them, too. They are coming quickly."

He lobbed another bomb and rode away from the barrier. The explosion was close enough to make him blink. Apparently, some of them had a shorter 'fuse.' Diego heard the guttural speech and saw several Resh spilling from inside the ship. Pulling out his stun rifle, Diego aimed and fired. There was a flash where his stun bolt hit the barrier, then dissipated. He berated himself for not remembering that no weapon would pass through a shield. Diego pulled back and waited to see what the Resh would do next. It paused, looking around, and then its bulbous eyes locked on his. Diego called out a Spanish expletive. His heels dug into Fuerte's side, and the reop leaped forward a few yards to draw them even farther from their ship.

Shield is down! That was Krim.

Diego aimed and fired. A warrior down. Then another. His count told him there were only four Resh left on the ship. "Attack!" He called on his communicator.

Krim, on the other reop, followed. When the brush became too thick, Diego halted and leaped off. He crept closer to the ship, drawn by the landing lights ahead. He admired the Resh for choosing this landing place — it offered excellent protection. Diego watched two Resh gathering up their belongings.

He fired and hit one. It howled and dropped the machine it carried, then wilted to the ground with a groan. The other Resh dashed toward the hatch. Krim hit it. The Resh collapsed without a sound. Before Diego could do more than blink, the hatch lowered, and the ship powered up. *Can one Resh fly that thing, or did I miscalculate how many were in there?* With a frustrated cry, he grabbed one of his remaining bombs and lobbed it. By a great stroke of luck, or maybe not luck, Diego thought later. It flew right through the sliver of space left as the hatch closed. The ship rose with a blast of heated air that drove Diego into the brush.

Then, a roar pushed him even deeper into the dirt and leaves. Burning bits of metal pelted him. Diego crawled back into the forest, fiery bits searing his back and singeing his hair. He heard a squeal of pain. "Fuerte! Krim!" A tree fell over in front of him. Diego crawled under the trunk. It was a little cooler, but he had to find Krim and Fuerte. Another, more muffled blast and then a crackling of burning brush. Fire!

"Diego!" Was that Rrishan?

"Diego! Commander?" Jeng? The communicator hissed too much to tell who was calling him. Diego kept crawling away. The ground was cool under his body, but he had to keep moving. Find the others. His back felt blistered and burned.

Jeng appeared. "Commander!"

"Where are Krim and Fuerte — the reops?"

"We have Krim in the land vehicle. Fuerte is nearby.

Rrishan is taking care of both."

Diego rose to his knees and then stood. He grabbed a sapling that was still standing. "The other bombs didn't cause that much damage."

Jeng shrugged. "Apparently, the bomb you threw into the ship was a more powerful one. We didn't have time to check and see if any were different."

Diego shook his head. "I can't believe we're still alive."

"Rrishan found a medical kit. We need to check you over."

"After Krim."

"Diego!" Rrishan called as Diego stumbled into the camp.

Then he saw Fuerte. Purplish-red blood dripped from many small wounds. Diego stepped closer, and the reop closed the gap. There was no limp, only hesitation, like exhaustion. Fuerte gave a snort and nuzzled his hand. Diego felt the muscular legs, the cloven hooves, shoulders, and chest. The wounds were small, and the blood already congealing. "Come, I'll get some water to wash off the dirt," he murmured.

"No, let me go to the stream and get the water so both you and Krim can get cleaned up," Rrishan said in no uncertain terms.

"How is Krim?"

"A tree fell on him and broke his arm, but he'll be all right. Just as you and Fuerte will with rest and medical attention. Will you please go sit down?"

Diego was too exhausted to argue with Rrishan. He sat down next to Krim. Jeng was working on her fellow Turengen's arm with supplies salvaged from their demolished spacecraft. Diego continued to watch Jeng work on Krim.

"What happened?" Jeng asked.

Diego shook his head. "Apparently, the last bomb was more powerful. I wanted to take the ship, not destroy it."

"Ship would not be taken, anyway. If you had not thrown the bomb inside, it would either be on its way to Resh, or after our comrades on the plains. I would rather destroy it," Jeng responded with Turengen logic.

"I suppose so, but we are still stranded."

Rrishan picked up the still unconscious Krim and carried him to the land crawler.

"We have a land vehicle," Jeng pointed out. "It is even big enough to hold the three reops."

"Three?"

Jeng shook her head. "Krim's reop didn't survive." She didn't elaborate, and Diego didn't ask.

CHAPTER THIRTY-EIGHT

"We need to see if we can find out anything from the surviving Resh before we leave," Diego said. "Can you get close enough to one to 'listen in' with none of them seeing you?"

"If we go out of our way to find them. It will delay us."

Diego sighed. Sometimes, he felt he depended on his comrades too much. "You're right. Let them think we're all dead. It will probably take a while for another ship to rescue them. Jeng, let's try to intercept Bress's party," Diego ordered. "As soon as we are able, we'll leave."

"Yes, Commander."

"I have Krim as comfortable as possible," Rrishan said. "He will rest easily in the bunk. Now it's time to check you out."

"I'm all right."

"I will determine that!" Rrishan huffed.

Diego gazed at her in surprise.

"Take off your protective suit."

"Huh?" *Strip in front of a girl?*

"I just want to see if the heat did any damage," Rrishan assured him. "The heat scorched your suit."

Diego pulled the all-weather suit down to the waist and shuddered at the sudden cold. He newly appreciated the outfits.

"Bruised all over. Skin's red, but the suit kept you from serious injury. Any place hurt?"

"No."

Rrishan slathered some kind of salve on his back that felt warm and tingly cold at the same time. Diego pulled on his travel suit again and, with Rrishan's help, doctored Fuerte. Then, he coaxed the reop through the hatch of the land vehicle. The other reops were skittish, but finally, with everyone helping and Fuerte nickering to them from inside, they entered and stood placidly beside Fuerte. Diego tied all three to the side of a bunk, hoping the trip wouldn't be too bumpy. He refilled the bucket with fresh water and found some of the moss and grass they liked to eat.

Fuerte nuzzled Diego, then grazed on a few bites. Again, Diego wondered why there were so few life forms on Nurisna. It made little sense. On his planet, there were rabbits, deer, and mice that ate the vegetation, coyotes eating the rabbits, wolves or cougars that ate or killed the coyotes. Humans killed or ate any of those. Many types of birds and creatures lived under the ground or in the water. There was hardly anything here. He shook his head and sat next to Rrishan, who sat in the pilot's chair. She glanced at him but said nothing.

"Let's find the rest of our crew."

Jeng took the seat right behind them. "This world is definitely a mystery, Commander."

"Yes, it is."

***

The sun rose as they headed south toward the place they felt Bress and the other Turengens might be. For a change, nothing impeded their journey. Diego glanced at the controls, trying to figure out the strange symbols.

"Jeng surmised the route the Hoorinoo and Bress's group took and figured out the Resh directional compass. We're heading toward the most logical meeting place."

"Good."

"It shouldn't take too long to find them," Jeng added.

Krim woke up when the sun was directly overhead. Jeng took over the controls, and the others took turns napping. It had been a long night. Diego tried to rest, but his mind churned with various worries. Occasionally, he cared for the reops, untangling their ropy manes and reassuring them.

"We are nearing the spot of rendezvous," Jeng announced. The engines powered down.

"One of us needs to meet them on foot," Diego pointed out. "I can take one of the reops." Diego led Fuerte through the hatch and down the ramp. Rrishan and Jeng led the others out. If the situation wasn't so serious, Diego might have found it humorous that a creature only slightly taller than thigh high was leading an animal as big as a reop.

In the bright sun, Diego examined Fuerte's wounds and knew it would be a while before he rode his reop. They had done a good job dressing the wounds, but Fuerte needed rest. Diego saddled another. "Rrishan, I will ride your reop. Fuerte still needs to recover," he said. The Grrlock helped him.

"Be careful, Diego…uh, Commander."

"I will, and you listen and watch for any Resh. Out here, there is no protection." He rode off. The gait of this reop differed from Fuerte's, but not anything he couldn't get used to. Rashti was also broader in the back and shoulders, so he adjusted his seat until he was comfortable. Just as Fuerte did, Rashti ran a mile-eating gallop. The taller hills rose in one direction, and the thick forests grew in another direction.

As he rode, he saw small, furred animals about the size of the rabbits of his world. These didn't hop. They scuttled. It was almost an hour before he caught any evidence of the other animals—small tracks showing through the prairie grasses. Rashti's round ears flicked, and she nickered, shaking her head and pulling to the right.

Diego gave the reop her head. She galloped in an easy lope until she reached a narrow stream. There, she stopped as though ready for a drink. There was no evidence of anyone, but Diego knew his friends were nearby. Then Bress walked out of the tall grass into the open. He chittered a greeting.

Diego laughed, more in relief than amusement. "Well met, Commander Bress! Where is everyone else?"

"Up ahead." The Turengen motioned for Diego to follow.

They didn't go far before Diego saw the others. He dismounted and greeted Hriffin. "Have you had any problems on your trek? Any Resh?"

"No," Hriffin said. "And you?"

While everyone sat down and rested, Diego called Rrishan on his communicator, giving her the coordinates. Then, he outlined what had happened.

"It is good, if you were not to capture the Resh ship, that you destroy it," Hriffin stated.

"That's what Jeng said. It won't take them long to meet us, and then most of us should be able to ride in the land vehicle."

"Commander, I wish to give you a report," Bress announced formally.

Diego nodded. "I need to let Rashti get a drink. You can give me your report there."

When they got to the stream, Bress said, "Shish, Prill, and Fress did well on this trek." He paused, then flicked his whiskers. "There is a mystery about this world."

"You noticed that, too?"

"Yes. I also notice Commander Perez is fretting too much about what has happened."

Diego bristled and then sighed. "I was really hoping to steal their ship so we would have a way off planet."

"There is much I was hoping, but I think there is something here more important than what we regret."

"What, Bress?"

"Why does this world has unlimited space and only two dominant forms of life?"

"I wondered that as well. It's a good thing the Hoorinoos and the reops are vegetarian, or they might be extinct."

"I think someone put them here to be farmed."

Diego stared at his second-in-command. "What?"

"I think neither is native to this world."

"Who would put them here?" Diego had his suspicions.

"I think either the Seressin or the Resh. Regardless, it's so long ago, the Hoorinoo don't remember coming from anywhere else."

"But Hrenssi said the Resh didn't know the females had a different pelt."

"It could be they really do but haven't been able to find the females until recently. There are many small mysteries in this big mystery, Commander. And I think the Hoorinoo have become superb at hiding. No one has detected them in their hill camps for a great length of time."

"What about the reops?" Diego was afraid he knew the answer to that question, too, but wanted confirmation.

"Food, especially for the Resh. Still, it is a theory, and I would have to talk to a Resh to test it."

"Phris was my teacher when I was first captured," Diego mused aloud. "So that would point to the Seressin."

"I believe both groups have visited Nurisna in the past centuries."

"And they both take slaves."

"True," Hriffin confirmed as he approached from a tall hummock of grass.

"Perhaps it is good I am stranded here. So, I am away from such a despicable practice."

Bress pulled on his whiskers. "What changes have happened in just the past solar turning — the past year?"

Diego looked at him, brows furrowed. "You mean gaining our freedom?"

"Yes. And we became commanders in a society almost completely reptilian for generations. If they continue to let you lead, you will change this society."

"You pin too much importance on me, Bress."

"No, you have shown them others have the same capabilities of greatness they have always believed only existed in their kind."

"A soft mammalian?" Diego said with a laugh.

"A soft mammalian." Bress chittered a short laugh.

"The Grrlocks were in command positions."

"A few were, but they got there slowly. The same with the Breanth and a few other species. There will be more now. Like our people."

Diego sighed. "I will reserve judgement."

"Keep an open mind."

They started back. "By the way, Hriffin, could my sub-commander's theory be right?"

Hriffin had been silent, listening. "I am not totally sure. There is no remembrance of such a thing, but it is very possible. We have dreams of darkness. Flying in darkness, in dark cocoons, then breaking out in sunlight. Like breaking out of an egg, except the cocoons were not eggs. The first parents were fully grown." Hriffin shrugged. "That is all we remember."

Diego started. It sounded like a version of Adam and Eve. "And the reops?" Diego asked, wondering if they came the same way the horses came in the New World.

"We saw a herd of them running across the edge of the prairie. Our ancestors captured some. It wasn't difficult. They have always been friendly."

"They should have overrun the prairie ecosystem with no natural enemy, but they don't seem very numerous," Bress continued. "That would support the theory they are here as a food source."

"We wondered the same thing," Hriffin explained. "They are not prolific, but they have their babies every year." By now, the rest of Hriffin and Bress's group had joined them.

"Definitely, there should be more." Diego sighed. "An

interesting problem, but right now, we need to stay out of the Resh's way. They'll be back."

CHAPTER THIRTY-NINE

"Will your people come to our planet to rescue you?" Hriffin inquired as they walked across the prairie.

Diego glanced at the Hoorinoo before answering. "I doubt it. If Marix Ziron was alive, I suspect he'd come eventually, but with him and the Supreme Commander dead, the empire is probably in chaos."

Bress trotted along beside Diego. "There is one thing I have pondered recently…"

"What?" Diego prompted when the Turengen hesitated.

"At the time of the explosion, I felt chaos of minds. I had to shut it off."

Diego waited.

"If all died…"

Diego understood the implications. "You wouldn't hear anybody! Are you saying the others are alive?"

Bress chittered something indistinct. "I have to admit, I don't know."

"But how?" Diego asked. "How could they still be alive?"

"Again, I don't know, but I think we need to get off this open grassland."

Rrishan met them with the land vehicle before they had walked too far. Most of the travelers managed to fit inside, although it was crowded. Diego rode Rashti, and Jeng and Bress rode the other reop. Rrishan didn't waste any time. She forced the vehicle into high gear and soon disappeared over the hill. Only the dust showed they were still nearby.

Diego kept thinking about what Bress said.

Bress communicated with him. *They are only guesses, Commander.*

Yes, I know. There is this — we still need to get the information on the Resh and their spiral energy ship back to Seress. We swore an oath.

We will prevail! He heard an undercurrent of Turengen humor in the declaration—as though Bress meant more than victory in battle.

***

The others had already set up camp near a small stand of trees when Diego and the two otter people caught up with them. Krim was up and about, although slowly. There was no fire, but several of the square stones had been set out. Hriffin leaned over one, and Diego led Rashti farther into the woods to take care of her. Jeng followed with her reop. Fuerte nickered and pulled away from the tree as they approached. He looked better. Diego pulled off Rashti's tack and brushed her with twigs and leaves. Rrishan brought a fresh container of water. Apparently, Fuerte was jealous. He nudged Diego and tried to snatch the twigs away.

Only when he finished did Diego pay attention to his friend. He checked each of Fuerte's scratches and cuts, then brushed him.

"Commander, you need to join the group," Bress said softly. "Hriffin wants to let you know what is going on with the rest of their people."

"Nothing bad, I hope."

"He has not said."

Diego followed Bress and sat down where Hriffin pointed—a place to the Hoorinoo's right. He waited.

"Hrenssi says ships patrol the air over the hills."

"Does she say how many?"

"She is not sure if one is doing a great deal of flying over the area or several are taking turns."

That would make it difficult to join them. "Can she tell if they are Resh or someone else?"

"No. And they have not been discovered as far as she knows. At least the ships haven't landed to investigate. Somehow, we need to get into the hills."

Diego rubbed his chin and thought. "Perhaps you could if there was a diversion."

"What kind of diversion?" Hriffin asked. "We already used a stampede as a diversion."

"But not one where the land vehicle is the bait."

"Bait?" Hriffin looked puzzled.

Instead of trying to explain, Diego smoothed out the soil in the middle of the circle and picked up a slender stick. "If we had the land vehicle in a position where it looked wrecked, they would land to investigate, wouldn't they?" He drew a crude picture of the lander as though it had fallen into a streambed. Diego drew several places where warriors hid in small holes in the ground or under thickets of dead limbs.

"A possibility," Bress answered.

"And if we were waiting in ambush, we could take the Resh, take their ship, and you Hoorinoo could make it to the hills." Diego sat back.

"Would they not be able to detect you and your people?" Hriffin asked.

"I hope they think we are all in the vehicle."

"Depends on how paranoid they are," Jeng said with a tug on her whiskers. "But I cannot think of anything else, Commander. That is the best plan we have."

"Another day before we come close to the foothills," Hriffin said.

"That's where we'll set it up. We'll separate before then. I think you need to hang back, Hriffin. We'll go ahead in the land vehicle, and your group can follow at your own pace, perhaps at night."

Within an hour, the Hoorinoos cut across the prairie almost parallel to the range of hills in the distance.

Diego hadn't asked about their travel plans. He figured the Hoorinoos had trekked this way for years and knew the best ways to go. Besides, what he didn't know, he wouldn't be able to tell the Resh. He slept near the vehicle, Fuerte standing over him.

The next morning, Diego and his crew took off. Rrishan announced they were getting low on fuel.

"Do you think we'll make it to the hills today?" Diego asked.

"I think so. Hard to read the Resh instruments, but the gauge seems to show we can go that far."

At midday, Diego and two of the Turengen mounted their reops and rode out to scout a place for an ambush. Diego watched Fuerte for a limp or re-opened wounds. He didn't let the reop travel at more than a slow gallop. Fuerte snorted his aggravation.

They hadn't ridden long before Rrishan's communicator warned them of activity in the air nine hundred schrechings, or three hundred miles, distant.

"Hold back until I give you word," Diego ordered. "We are going to find a place to set up our surprise."

After riding closer to the foothills, Diego began thinking nothing would look convincing. Then, they found a small river that had dug out a deep course in the soft soil. Diego rode down to the stream and dismounted. He studied the soil. "As good as we can ask for. Dig out here, and there, and over there on the other side. I'll look for branches or something to further camouflage our hiding places." He called Rrishan and ordered her to rendezvous.

"It is primitive enough to surprise the Resh," Bress observed. He pulled off his pouch loaded with weaponry and, using a sturdy branch from the river, dug a short tunnel within a brief time.

The Turengen's skill amazed Diego. He began digging his tunnel when he realized one of their hiding places needed to be above the bank. Diego climbed and studied the area. Not too far away, he found a small depression that, with not too much work, would be big enough for him to hide. There wasn't much in the way of branches or debris to hide under. Diego dug out several large rocks and pushed them in front of his place of ambush. It would have to do.

Now, he had to consider the reops. He pulled off Fuerte's tack and motioned for him to run away. The reop gazed at him, softly nickering.

"Let me try," Bress offered. "This was how we coaxed them into letting us ride them." The Turengen stared into the animal's eyes. After a few minutes, Fuerte snorted and then turned and ran back into the prairie. The other two reops followed.

"Stay safe," Diego whispered.

Bress patted Diego on the arm. "Rrishan will soon be here. She says the Resh have detected her."

"How long will we have to set the ambush up?"

"Perhaps two macro-cycles."

Diego translated. About an hour. "Tell her to bring it in fast, then stop before the actual riverbank."

Bress gazed at Diego's hiding place. "I will get Jeng to come and make this more camouflaged."

"It's a rather bad job, isn't it?"

"No, we are just better at digging."

Diego laughed. "You're better at almost everything."

"You are a better leader."

By the time Rrishan appeared on the horizon, Diego had figured out the exact place to stage the "accident."

"I think they have figured out we're not their warriors," she said over the communicator.

"Bress, can you pick up her thoughts?"

"Barely."

"Rrishan, get off the communicator!"

There was a brief buzz and then silence. "Tell her to come in fast. I'll signal when to slow down. There's rock down here where we may pull the vehicle out when this is all over." Diego pointed.

Bress seemed to concentrate, and then he nodded. "She heard. And will be here soon."

Diego saw puffs of dust before seeing the land explorer. The puffs became billows, and then he saw the machine. He waved and pointed. The vehicle stirred up more debris as she put on the brakes. Rrishan eased closer and stopped at the edge. It was a four-foot drop. Diego motioned for her to move forward.

She did, and the explorer tilted over the bank. Sand and gravel slid down, and so did the land explorer. With the nose stuck in the dirt just in front of the river, Rrishan powered down the engine.

"Tell her to keep it on."

Bress did so.

"She needs to bring a few explosives. We're going to put traps on the outside."

"My people can ambush from the river."

Rrishan and the Turengen hauled out all their explosives. Fress remained inside, monitoring the approach of the Resh ship.

"Is this thing going to survive?" Rrishan asked.

"Probably not, but it's the ship we need," Diego said.

"And if we don't?"

"If we don't, what? Survive or get the ship?"

She gave a soft hiss, then smiled. "Get the ship."

"Then we're no worse off than we were before."

"Ship coming in fast. Communications are Resh," Fress chittered before leaping into the river.

"If you're waiting in the river, get back from the vehicle. Rrishan, come with me," Diego ordered. He dashed up the opposite bank and crawled under the brush. Rrishan was right behind him. The Turengen had done a terrific job. The scream of an incoming ship had him scanning the far horizon through the branches. The ship seemed to come right at him, it flew so low. Then it fired, and the river exploded.

CHAPTER FORTY

The land vehicle, as well as everything around it, blasted into chunks of metal, dirt, rocks, and water. The scream changed into coughing roars as the ship flew away. Could the attacking ship have been hit? There was no smoke, but the Resh vessel careened lower and slower as it soared away. Then before it flew totally out of sight. It slewed into the ground, throwing up dirt and vegetation far into the sky.

"What?"

"He came in too low and got caught in our hastily set up explosions. I think he misjudged how the vehicle would explode, too," Rrishan said with a yowling laugh.

"The Turengen!" Diego cried. He ran to the bank and slid down. Water splashed against either bank, dyed brown with mud—he hoped it was mud. *Krim! Bress! Jeng! Shish! Fress! Prill!* He waded in.

"Will search!" Jeng called out, sliding down from her cave. She and Bress dove into the water.

Diego churned around in the opaque water, reaching in and trying to feel for any bodies. Something bumped against his leg. He grabbed and pulled. Prill. Diego pulled him to the shore, where Rrishan checked him over. Bress hauled someone else out—Fress. Jeng dove back into the river after rescuing one of her companions.

"Who's missing?" he called.

"Shish," Bress chittered.

Diego slipped and fell into the deeper part of the river. He floundered a minute and then got his footing. The current tried to yank him underwater, but he grabbed onto a large rock and pulled himself to his feet, then to the shore. He waded over to Rrishan. "How are they?"

"I'm worried about Fress. She is having trouble breathing."

Diego made his way to the stricken Turengen. Then he reached around her furry middle and pushed his fist into her diaphragm, something Commander Hreeshan taught him. She coughed up water and then sucked in air. He did it again. Finally, she opened her eyes, hacking and chittering. Diego sat back and watched her.

"Com…mander," she wheezed.

"Can you breathe all right?"

Fress spat water. "Yes."

"Prill has a huge lump on his head, but he seems to be breathing all right," Rrishan reported.

The other two Turengen coughed and choked but were doing better. Diego gazed at the river, hoping to see Bress and Jeng hauling Shish out. He didn't see any of them. Diego sat on the bank amid the pieces of metal, rock, and sand and kept watching.

"What about the Resh ship?" Rrishan asked.

As much as he worried about the Turengens, he needed to see if they had to deal with Resh. "I'll reconnoiter."

"Not without at least one other person!" Rrishan grabbed a pistol.

Diego nodded. "Fress, do you feel like taking care of Prill and Krim?"

"Yes."

Diego scrambled up the bank. Dust rose in the distance, but there was a small amount of smoke. Rrishan followed in silence.

As they drew near the ship, the pair separated and approached from either side. Diego bent low in the waving grasses, occasionally straightening and watching for activity. A low whine and then several clicks told him the hatch was opening. He moved closer to the ship, almost running until he was near enough to see clearly.

The door ground open, but no ramp extended. A Resh peered out, watching the waving grass. It shot into the vegetation, hitting about twenty feet to his left. A guttural order came from inside, and the rifle lowered. The warrior still maintained watch. Diego did as well.

Found Shish? Diego thought to the searching Turengens.

No. We are coming to help.

Hopefully, Shish was downstream a short distance, and she would return soon. Jeng showed up at his side. Diego didn't have to point out the Resh warrior. Another appeared at the hatch. They climbed out, their rifles ready. *How many?*

Hard to tell. Some thoughts blare, and some are like whispers. Maybe eight or ten.

Those weren't the greatest odds, but not insurmountable. Diego waited. Another warrior jumped out with a bulky-looking contrivance on his back. He felt uneasy about this. The contrivance had a narrow hose attached to the butt end of his rifle.

They're going to burn the grassland! Jeng shouted in his mind.

"Tell the others to retreat to the river. Go!" Diego hissed. He backed away as he spoke. Jeng turned tail and dashed into the grass. Diego wanted to keep a watch on the Resh but couldn't stay too long. If they set the grass on fire, his warriors wouldn't be able to get close to the ship. For all he knew, the Resh would only need to make quick repairs and then take off.

Diego wondered if he could damage the weapon. He stood, aimed, and fired. The laser hit the backpack. It exploded, and the Resh screamed, jerking off the blazing pack. Unfortunately, it slid just inside the hatch. A half dozen toad people leaped out of the ship, screaming in fear.

"Bress, Rrishan, get back here!" he shouted, then ran forward, zigzagging to avoid the weapon's fire from all the Resh that had evacuated their ship. One of them tried to leap back in, but Diego fired his rifle, grazing him. He gave a croaking scream and fell.

With speed he didn't know he had, Diego reached the ship. "Drop your weapons!" he called in Seressin.

One of them did. The others looked for Diego's backup, didn't see any, and then raised their rifles. A shot from the grass dropped one of the Resh warriors, and the rest threw their weapons down. Rrishan rose, her growl fierce.

One of the Resh—Diego assumed he was the leader— croaked an order. A warrior stooped to pick up his weapon, but another shot threw the creature backward into the grass, unconscious.

Diego walked closer, motioning for the Resh to move away from the spaceship and their rifles. The Turengen came out of hiding as well—all of them except Bress.

"Watch them closely. I will check out the ship. There could be another inside."

Don't believe there is anyone still in the ship; I can't feel anyone else, Bress told him.

Diego climbed inside. The main cabin appeared intact, although there would be no way to determine if it was spaceworthy until they could check out all the systems. He reconnoitered all the rooms, anywhere a Resh might hide. Diego turned back to the hatch when he heard shouts outside.

Bress trotted down the corridor. "I will finish checking the ship, Commander. You need to take care of our prisoners."

"What in the world are we going to do with them?"

Bress grinned. "Take them to Seress if this ship will fly."

"Nine of them?"

"No. Six. One was already dead, and we had to shoot two who tried to kill us."

Diego scratched behind his ear. "I didn't see a jail or brig, so I think we'll have to use one of the cargo holds."

"I will check, Commander. The leader has a translator. Speak big."

"Big?" Then he realized he needed to act tough. "Oh, all right." Diego stood in the hatch and studied the Resh prisoners. Five glowered at him, and one of them lay unconscious in the grass. "Who has the translator?"

"I have a translator, but I also know Seressin language, as grotesque as it is," the largest Resh said.

"Can I presume you are the captain of this ship?"

The Resh paused a moment before speaking. "Yes, I am. Why am I speaking to a mammalian youth? Where is the commander of your invasion party?"

"You are speaking to the commander. I am Commander Diego Perez."

The Resh laughed, a gurgling, hiccupping sort of sound.

Diego waited for him to pause for breath. "I am also known as Moon Crusher."

The Resh captain swallowed his laugh. "You joke."

"No, I don't. And I didn't joke when my crew and I destroyed several Resh battle cruisers in the Koressian system."

"What are you doing here?" the captain demanded.

Diego frowned. "You demand nothing from me. I demand. You are my prisoner. I will ask the questions."

"I do not have to answer them."

"That is your choice, Captain." He turned to Rrishan. "You, Prill, and Fress watch the prisoners. Put your settings on stun and shoot them if they give you a hard time. Jeng and Bress, shall we check out the ship?"

Jeng pattered through the control room, stopping to activate various systems. Bress joined her. Diego went into the cargo hold and checked out the feasibility of keeping the Resh prisoners there. He wished they could chain them to the wall. Then, he wouldn't be worrying about them while they traveled to Seress. Better yet, give them something to knock them out for the duration of their trip. He returned to the control room.

"Spaceworthy?" Diego asked Jeng, who worked under a console.

"You are too impatient, Commander," Jeng replied, her voice muffled. "Will tell you as soon as I can."

"Sorry."

"No problem, sir. I want to go back, too."

Diego wondered whether any of them had a family to return to.

Bress slid out from behind the main computer. "Computers are online again. I will run a systems check for the entire ship now. Maybe you and Fuerte can look for Shish?"

"Yes, we need to find her." When he left the spaceship, Diego saw the Turengen had the situation well in hand. They restrained their Resh prisoners with a variety of materials — rope, straps, and wires.

"All under control, Commander," Krim answered before Diego could say anything.

"Good." He didn't have to tell them what he planned to do. Diego walked toward the river, wondering if the reops were anywhere nearby. At the bank, he studied the scene of chaos. Softly eddying water filled the crater where the land explorer had blown up. The rest of the water rushed downstream, foaming over lichen-covered rocks and debris.

Diego whistled. He hadn't trained the deer-horse creature to come on a whistle command because he didn't need to. Fuerte seemed to know when he needed him. Sometimes, he whistled to reassure the animal. He whistled again, the sound piercing the noise of the river. After a few moments, Diego felt the ground shiver beneath his boots. He thought he heard thunder in the distance. Diego looked toward the sky, but there were no clouds. Earthquake?

Then, he saw a cloud of dust. Watching, Diego spied a herd of animals rushed toward him. The only animals he knew large enough to make so much noise and dust were reops.

He saw Fuerte in front of a large herd. They all stopped about ten feet ahead of him. Diego only recognized a few of them. *Where had the others come from?* At least forty animals stared at him. Fuertes stepped closer and pushed Diego's chest with his nose. With a laugh, Diego scratched under his friend's chin. He found the saddle pad and bridle and put them back on. "What are we going to do with your friends?"

Some reops wandered in the grass, grazing. Others continued to watch him. Diego mounted and guided Fuerte downstream. If they followed, they followed. Diego left the communicator open as he searched. A few of the reops followed, but most stayed back and grazed. Diego kept to a trot, studying the water. Finally, Diego saw something that clashed with the surrounding rocks and dirt.

Dismounting, Diego slid down the bank and to the river's edge. There, he found Shish. He checked for breath. She was dead. He pulled her farther out of the water and carried her up the bank. Mounting awkwardly with the limp body in his arms, Diego galloped toward the Resh ship. It didn't take long. Fress greeted him; her eyes were darker than usual.

"I'm sorry."

"You found her. We can make the farewell," she replied, pointing to a place under a flowering bush.

Fuerte didn't need coaxing. He walked over to the squat bush. Diego slid off and lay the dead Turengen down. By now, her pelt was dry, and she looked as though she slept. Diego felt the deaths of so many. He turned away before his thoughts became too depressing.

CHAPTER FORTY-ONE

He returned to the ship on reop-back. The Resh captain stared and then laughed. "You ride food?

Fuerte snorted as he came to a halt. "I ride transportation," Diego replied. "I ride an animal I treat with respect, just as I did back on my home planet."

"You rode food on your home planet?"

Diego pictured riding a steer and smiled. "No." He dismounted and entered the scout ship.

"Commander!" Bress announced. "The ship's hull integrity is sound, fuel intact, as is life support and all other necessary systems."

"Wonderful!"

"A few systems need work, and we need to replenish the food supplies. I don't think we want to rely on Resh rations." Bress chittered a laugh.

Diego joined him. "Considering they use reops as a food source, I agree. What systems need work?"

Jeng took over the explanations. "Navigation suffered some damage during the landing. One of the landing struts broke, so that will make it difficult to take off. Some weapons systems are damaged. We would be in a great deal of danger if we ran across either Resh or Seressin."

"Defensive shields?"

Jeng replied, "I think they are all working fine, but can

only test them once we are space borne."

Diego was eager to get away and back to Seressin. "Can we be ready to leave in three-day cycles?"

"Difficult, but I think we can do it," Bress replied.

"Good."

"And the prisoners, Commander?"

"We take the command crew, strip the others, and leave them behind," Diego replied.

Bress pointed from the open hatch. "What about the reops?" The other animals straggled into sight.

"Obviously, we can't take them with us, despite the Resh considering them food."

"Perhaps we can bring the ones we have trained."

"If the Seressin or Grrlocks see them as a viable transplant species, others can be rescued later."

Jeng cocked his head. "Why would a race as advanced as the Seressin, Grrlock, or Breanth even consider something as primitive as riding a reop?"

"Because they're quiet, fast, and loyal. They're smart, too," Rrishan interjected. "And I like them."

Diego couldn't help it; he smiled. Horses, reops, they grew on you. As much as he had experienced in the past year plus, Diego still missed horses. Still missed the feel of vibrant muscles between his legs. Reops were the substitute and, in some ways, even better than horses. Taking Fuerte would also prevent his guilt at leaving his friend on a hostile planet while he shot off to safety. "You mentioned some deficiencies in the food supply?"

"You gave most to the Hoorinoos," Jeng pointed out.

"We will fish and collect some of the fruit Hriffin pointed out. How long will it take to get to a Seressin controlled planet?" Diego asked.

"Next system beyond," Bress pointed out. "Both empires have contested this one for many years. It will take perhaps two days."

"Good." Diego said nothing about Shish.

"We will say farewell to Shish tonight as the sun descends," Bress said.

"Let me know what you'd like me to do." Diego nodded.

***

To Diego's delight, the ship was ready in three days. Jeng had changed the command controls so that they responded to the Turengen. They had partitioned a space in the cargo hold for three reops and four Resh prisoners. The crew tested the ship's lifters by pulling it out of the hole it had gouged during landing. It stood crookedly on the three landing legs that remained intact, but it stood. Diego opted to give the Resh a sedative Krim had found in the medical bay. He worried about the reops and considered staying in the bay with them during take-off.

"Let me, Commander. I can communicate well with them," Fress said.

"You'll be all right?"

"Of course. You belong in the control room."

Diego reassured Fuerte and then headed into the top-level control area. He sat in the command chair, feeling anything but commanding. "Let's get out of here," he ordered. Then added a more formal, "Take us out."

Bress engaged the engines slowly in deference to the damaged landing gear. When the ship was high enough off the ground, he engaged the aft thrusters, and they shot into the air. Life support kept gravity forces reasonable.

Diego watched the monitor. The light lavender sky darkened, then changed to black. Stars appeared, glowing steadily. It never ceased to amaze him — how much more beautiful the stars were in space rather than watching from the ground. "Shortest route to Seressin territory."

"Yes, Commander."

"And be ready with identification."

"Yes, sir."

Diego worried that someone would prefer to destroy their ship as opposed to asking questions first.

There were no problems leaving the Nuriss System. Rrishan and Prill detected no ships near either of the fold gates. Diego drummed the armrest of this chair. He got up and approached navigation. "I have the class five codes if there is a Seressin ship on the other side."

Diego watched the approaching fold gate on Bress's monitor. A soft circular glow indicated the passage to the Seressin Empire. Diego noted the diminishing distance and realized he was holding his breath. He let it out, pulled in another one, and did a quick relaxation mantra before gripping the back of Bress's seat even harder.

"Approaching."

"Be ready," Diego added.

The chime of impending shift and then the quick discomfort. There wasn't even time to feel the inside-out sensation before the ship was rattled with a near blast.

"Shields!" Diego called out.

"They were up. That was a big blast!" Krim replied.

"Who's out there?" Diego asked Prill. "And take evasive action."

The monitor showed the stars slewing around, but the artificial gravity kept everything on an even keel.

"Identify without codes first!"

"Yes, Commander," Bress said. He typed the identification of their ship. In a few words, he added the circumstances of their being in a Resh ship.

"Open the audio."

Bress typed some more and then made a motion to Diego.

"This is Sub-Commander Diego Perez...."

He couldn't finish. Another blast caused the lights to flicker and the systems to 'hiccup.'

"They are Seressin, sir!" Prill shouted.

Diego sat down next to Bress and reached over to the communications console. He typed in the codes Marix Ziron had given him so long ago. With a sigh, he sat back and waited.

"A message, Commander."

"Put it on, Prill." There were no more blasts.

The voice over the communicator spoke Seressin. "You will disengage your sub-light and post-light engines. Lower your defensive shields and await boarding by Seressin authority."

Diego answered. "We will disengage engines, but we will not lower shields until you are ready to board."

"Lower your shields, or we will blast your ship into dust!"

"Do that, and you'll not have the pleasure of interrogating our Resh prisoners," Diego replied in a calm voice.

There was a long pause, and then, "Prepare to be boarded. We will inform you when we are in boarding posture."

"Very well, Commander."

They waited. Diego paced, then realized how useless that was. "Bress, I will be back before they can enter. I want to see how our cargo fared. You have temporary command."

Diego strode down the corridor, slid down the stairway, and entered the cargo bay. Fuerte nickered. The other two reops pranced. Fress sat beneath one of the reop's legs, stroking the coarse pelt. Diego figured that was unorthodox, but it seemed to work. The reop was a little less skittish. The Resh were still asleep in the opposite corner. Diego stroked Fuerte's nose and under his jaw. "You'll be all right. Soon, our trip will be over. Good work, Fress."

She grinned and chittered, continuing to stroke the nervous reop.

"The Seressin are ready to board, Commander," Bress informed him over the communicator.

Diego sprinted to the cargo room hatch. Prill and Krim joined him. Diego worked the controls, watching the pressure dials. Four suited figures entered the outer hatch and then waited while the air recycled into the small room. They all had weaponry attached to their harnesses. When pressure equalized, Diego punched the inner lock control, and the heavy door ground open. As they walked out of the hatch, they had their weapons drawn and ready.

The foremost Seressin pressed a button on the front of his suit and then pulled off his helmet, handing it to Krim. The Turengen stared in surprise.

Diego gasped and then stammered, "Wel... Welcome aboard, Commander." He couldn't believe he was staring at Commander Hreeshan. "But you were...dead!"

"Dead?" The Grrlock yowled soft laughter.

CHAPTER FORTY-TWO

"Uh, yes sir! I mean, yes, Commander. We saw the ship explode."

"No, Diego, you saw an explosion. A big one, amplified by our computers to look like a much larger ship had exploded."

The implications of that sped through his mind. "Then Marix Ziron? Rreengrol? Everybody on the *Star Devourer*?"

"All alive—and well. Sub-commander Rreengrol and I have been freed of the Resh programming. They cannot do that again. All the outlying systems of the empire are under heightened alert. We are part of a patrol to make sure the Resh do not infiltrate again," Hreeshan said with a growl.

The other three warriors took off their helmets. Commander Lurin handed Prill his helmet with a grumble about claustrophobic metal bird cages. The other two were Seressin warriors Diego didn't know. He grinned and then gave a whoop that reverberated down the corridor.

"Come, let's go into the control room and get this bucket to Seress. The War Department will love going over this," Lurin ordered. "I am assuming you returned my Turengen warriors back to me in one piece?"

"Except for Shish, sir. We lost her in battle," Diego reported.

"Sorry to hear that. Great warriors. Great techs."

"Yes, sir. I hope the Supreme Commander will use the information about a new ship the Resh have invented. I don't know if you can get much information from the Resh captain and his subordinates, but we brought them along, too."

Hreeshan nodded. "The Commander has been worried about you ever since you took off in his ship through a fold portal. I think you live a sreching blessed life. Some star likes you."

"Sir, I had a crew...."

Lurin boomed, "Of course you did. And they like you, too! You are loyal to them and them to you."

Hreeshan grinned. "We will let the Marix know you and your crew are all right, and then you can tell me what happened."

***

When the ship landed in Marix Ziron's landing bay, the Seressin commander was waiting to greet them. Ziron closed the distance to Diego. He was flattered, flustered, and totally relieved. Ziron thumped him on the back and dragged him off to a private banquet for his commanders. Rrishan's look told him the reops would be cared for.

"I have heard some almost unbelievable things, Quirlis. That you took my ship to the Resh home system and rescued a Turengen and a Grrlock."

Even though he had already completed a report for Marix Ziron, Diego related what he and the Turengen had done. "We were fortunate, too, Marix."

"By the stars and the comet, you have fortune to be envied!" Ziron cried. He toasted his squire's success. "You know there are rewards for such exploits."

"Yes, sir, but I don't need any money rewards."

"Never hurts to have something put away."

"I know, sir. There are two things I would like, though, if you could grant me permission for them."

"And they are?" Ziron asked, his red eyes glinting in humor.

"My first teacher—Phris, the Hoorinoo. Could he be freed so he could join his people?"

Ziron rubbed under his chin. "I can't imagine that a small

slave like that would be all that expensive."

Diego cringed but hid it. "Thank you, Marix."

"And what else?"

"Could I take a cargo ship and gather more of the reops? The Grrlock leadership said they had plenty of space for an orphan species to thrive."

"I can do better than that, Diego. We sent an expeditionary force to claim the Nuriss System. Our forces are building several outposts to keep watch for Resh incursions."

"That's wonderful, Marix. Then, can my second request be that the Hoorinoos be granted free settler status? That they are not taken as slaves anymore?"

"What about teachers? They are invaluable for that," Marix said with a fixed gaze at his squire.

Diego blushed. "Um, you could hire them, sir."

"Hire them?"

"Yes, sir."

"I will definitely have to rethink how we run our ships."

"Sir, if a worker had some promise that with hard work they could advance out of slavery, I believe they should be better workers." The other commanders were listening, some appearing disdainful and others ambivalent.

"You being the perfect example?"

"Yes, Marix. And the Turengen, too."

"I will think on the proposal. It has merit. However, don't push for too much, too quickly, Quirlis."

"No, sir."

"But with that idea in mind, do you think the Hoorinoos might be interested in being part of a warrior force on Nurisna?"

Diego had to work hard to keep the grin off his face. "One could only ask, sir, but I think they might like that. Especially with the aid of the reops. They have learned to ride them."

Ziron nodded. "Then I would like you to take that proposal to them. It is from the Supreme Commander."

"I would be honored. And may I take Phris?"

"Of course, since you freed him. I trust you to pick your own delegation."

Diego didn't squelch the grin this time. "Thank you, Marix Ziron."

"Oh, and you are officially no longer my squire."

"Sir?"

"No, you are on my staff as a mid-grade sub-commander."

"Marix?"

"Don't make me regret it! And don't look so surprised. You'll still be learning in between official duties. Go get ready for your assignment!"

"Yes, sir!" Diego gave the Seressin salute—thumb to forehead, then to chest, bowed, and he left the room. It was good to be back home.

Susan Kite was born in Indiana, but because her father was in the Army, she moved extensively during her growing up years. The post library was the first place she found after a move, avidly reading fantasy, science fiction, and many other genres. In her teens, she dabbled in writing, creating stories based on characters from her favorite TV shows. With college and marriage, writing was mostly put on hold.

That changed more than twenty years ago when the writing bug bit again. For a decade, fan fiction was the main focus, but this provided practice and helped develop skills needed to write original works. A visit to the Mission San Luis Rey in California in 2001 and subsequent research became the catalyst to write her first novel, *My House of Dreams*. *The Mendel Experiment*, and its sequels, *Blue Fire, and Power Stone of Alogol*, were published by World Castle.

The author earned her Bachelor's degree in secondary English and followed that up with a Master's degree in Instructional Media at Utah State University. She worked in public school libraries for 35 years, most recently in Chattanooga, Tennessee.

Now retired, Ms. Kite lives in Oklahoma City. She has been married to the love of her life, Daniel, for over 40 years. They have two children and seven grandchildren and are owned by an opinionated chiweenie-terrier.